MOTHER OF DARKNESS

CARNIVAL OF TERROR SERIES

BOOK 2

IAN FORTEY
AND
RON RIPLEY

EDITED BY ANNE LAO
AND DAWN KLEMISH

Enter the Realm of Terror...

We'd like to take a moment to thank you for your support and invite you to join our VIP newsletter.

Dive deeper into the darkness with exclusive offers, early access to new releases, and bone-chilling deals when you sign up at www.ScareStreet.com.

Let the nightmares begin...

See you in the shadows,
Scare Street

PROLOGUE

Screams upon screams filled the night. The lights were flashing like a thousand fireflies and the air felt electric. This was fun. This was intense. This was thrills and scares and exhilaration.

People rarely felt more alive than in moments of great fear. That was why many loved rollercoasters and racing cars and skydiving and all of those things. It was like laughing in the face of death. That you could come close to something dangerous and maybe even feel, deep down, that you were helpless. It was freeing.

Of course, there was not supposed to be genuine fear. Not from a roller coaster. Not from the height of a Ferris wheel. Not from the freaks in a freakshow. They were scary in a controlled and easily digestible way. For that reason, the fear became transformative. Cathartic, even. It was fun. Fear and terror could be a person's goal. And they craved it.

But genuine fear— the kind no one signed up for, the kind that surprised a person and that had no safeguards—well, that was different. That fear didn't end in laughs. Those screams were all too real.

Wendell didn't understand those thrill-seekers. The carnival wasn't like a theme park with crazy rides, but the freakshow and the Ferris wheel gave it elements of danger and horror. The Ferris wheel was the most rickety, dangerous thing he'd seen in his life. If it could legally pass a safety inspection, he'd marry a goat.

As for the freakshow, it could have been worse. He'd learned that people had quit recently. That was why so many new hires like him were coming on. A change in management led to a lot of older workers quitting. The freakshow was down to a strongman, conjoined twins, a sword swallower, and some jars that held deformed animals and fetuses.

For Wendell, fear was an unwanted emotion. He enjoyed having fun as much as anyone, but not if it was going to lead to white-knuckle panic and nightmares. The local fools could have that any day of the week and twice on Sunday, as far as he was concerned.

Wendell had joined the carnival because he needed work and he liked deep-fried foods; it was as simple as that. He had nothing tying him down, so travel wasn't an issue. They didn't require any special skills, and they offered more than minimum wage. It was a good deal.

The work wasn't easy, so every cent he got was well-earned. He had no idea the labor that went into setting up, maintaining, and then taking down a carnival. It was constantly slogging. Lifting and carrying and adjusting and moving. And they were so short-staffed since everyone quit that all the work was on the shoulders of the few laborers—which the owner insisted on calling roustabouts—on hand.

When the carnival was in full swing, that was ironically Wendell's most laid-back time. It meant everything was set up and running and his job was done. He could take time to enjoy the fruits of his labor, which he did.

Wendell was a sucker for games, especially the shooting gallery. He never took prizes, of course, but the guy who ran the game, Sherman, loved him. Wendell was a crack shot and hit the target ninety-nine times out of a hundred. He was good for business and could draw a crowd by making trick shots. People watched him shoot and then paid for their chance.

He got a kick out of the kids who were impressed by his marksmanship, and also the odd couple where Wendell could show up the guy in front of his old lady. He only did that if the guy seemed like a jerk, or if his girl was especially pretty. Other times, he'd throw a challenge and let the guy win if he seemed like he needed it. Or if he slipped Wendell a twenty ahead of time. Wendell was pretty easy to work with.

"Hey, buddy."

Wendell turned as he walked past one of the food booths on the small midway. The man in the nearest booth gave him a quick wave.

"Yeah?" Wendell asked.

"You're one of the new guys, right? Grab me another sugar box?"

"Sugar box?" Wendell asked. The man nodded and held up an empty box.

"For the cotton candy machine. This town loves the stuff, and I only got one left in here. They should be in the supply truck," the man said.

Wendell nodded, dropping his plans to go play a quick ring-toss game, and veered right. He could cut through the freakshow tents and slip out the back of the carnival to where the trucks were parked. He wasn't sure which one was the supply truck since there were a half-dozen lined up, but he'd figure it out.

The carnival trucks were beyond the tents. The lights were all fixed toward the carnival, and the line of silent vehicles was almost like a maze to navigate in the dark. He made his way through the backs of three trucks, finding nothing food-related and beginning to question whether he needed to go back and ask the cotton candy guy for more specific directions.

When he was hired barely a month ago, Wendell's interview process with Mr. Hartwell mostly amounted to asking if he could lift more than fifty pounds and if he had any family or friends waiting for him.

The second question seemed odd until Hartwell explained that constantly being on the road meant not seeing friends and family, and he'd lost a lot of employees to homesickness. He needed to be sure no one was waiting for Wendell. No one was.

Wendell had been on his own since he was about fifteen. He had to have a father somewhere, but he didn't know the man's name or anything else about him. He had doubts about whether his mom even knew who he was.

His mother had been in and out of jail for most of Wendell's childhood. His aunt raised him for a spell, and then, his grandmother. All three women were gone now. His mother had overdosed three days after her last release date. Grandma had passed when she was eighty-nine, and his aunt had died in a car crash. There was no one left.

He bounced between friends' houses and the streets for a while and eventually got a job in construction that let him get his own place. When the business hit a slump, he did odd jobs here and there and kept his head above water. It was lonely though.

Staying away from drugs—both using and selling—was hard. He had lots of opportunities, but he wanted to live his life straight. He wanted to prove he could succeed where his mother had failed. And while he couldn't say he'd succeeded at anything in life, he hadn't failed, either. He was doing the best he could. It was hard, but it worked.

The carnival was a good opportunity for him. With nothing tying him down in life, he didn't have a lot of expenses. And he could stay in the carnival trucks with other workers, so he didn't have rent and other bills. They even made communal meals, and all he had to do was chip in a few bucks a week and help with cooking and cleaning to be part of it. It was cool.

He didn't think he was making lifelong friends at Bartolomy and Sons' Carnival and Sideshow. He still barely knew anyone's name. But it didn't matter. If he worked hard, they didn't give him a hard time. He had fun hustling games, and he was getting to travel across the country. He could think of worse jobs.

Wendell reached the next truck in the line and took hold of the rear door latch. He gave it a half turn and then pulled, lifting the loading door straight up. The air that rolled out at him was hot and damp and positively vile.

He stumbled back, trying to stifle the vomit that rose in his throat. The stench was like nothing he'd ever experienced, something rotten and horrible. He had to turn his back on the truck to find a patch of fresh air.

After a handful of breaths to steady himself and quell the urge to vomit, he looked back. It was dark and impossible to see what the problem was, but there was definitely something wrong. The truck must have accidentally been packed with raw meat, or maybe a raccoon climbed in and died or something.

Wendell pulled his cell phone from his pocket, activated the flashlight app, and lifted it. His hand shook as the beam filled the rear of the truck.

Bodies were stacked on top of each other. There were dozens, piled up like anything else being loaded for transport. They sat in a pool of stagnant runoff, a dark liquid that must have been old, congealed blood, and the slurry of other things that leak from a corpse over time.

Some bodies looked relatively fresh, maybe days old. Others were weeks old, bloated and purple and covered in disfiguring marks. He couldn't see all the faces, but many looked to have been burned, with black scars that obscured their identity, made worse by the conditions in which they were being stored.

They weren't all facing the same direction, but Wendell recognized some of them. He saw the old fortune teller, Shiva, who had quit just after he was hired. He only knew this by her clothes and hair, as her face had already rotted off.

He recognized a few others, roustabouts and game runners and even a pair of freaks from the freakshow. He was told they'd all quit or run off because they didn't like the management shift and were loyal to the old crew.

He recognized some of the newer ones as well. Not workers, but customers, people he had seen in passing. He didn't know them, but they were familiar.

"Jesus," Wendell gasped from behind the veil of his shirt. It did little to hide the stench, but he still felt better holding it up. Like it somehow protected him from whatever happened to all the dead bodies in that truck.

"What the hell are you doing?"

The voice made Wendell jump, the shirt pulling away from his face. He turned to see Mr. Hartwell, the carnival's new owner. He still wore his silly-looking top hat, but in the dark, in the stink of death, it didn't look funny at all.

"Jesus, Mr. Hartwell, there's—"

"You shouldn't be here!" Hartwell snapped, cutting him off.

He didn't care about the truck full of corpses. Wendell quickly understood what was happening. Hartwell knew about the truck. He didn't care that it was full of dead bodies, he just cared that someone had found it. Wendell's stomach dropped.

"I won't tell anyone," Wendell whispered. It was a lie, but he would say or do anything he could to survive. He would not be the next body in that truck.

"You can't be here!" the older man said, looking around them.

The statement caught him off-guard. He took a step back and Hartwell locked eyes on him again. Even in the shadows, he could sense that Hartwell wasn't expressing rage. He was terrified.

"Mr. Hartwell?"

"Run, goddamn you. Run as fast as you can."

Wendell raised his hands and took a step back. The air grew chilly around him, and Hartwell moaned, turning his head away.

"No. You can't keep doing this," he said, his tone pleading and sad.

Wendell took another step back and stopped as something cold like ice fell on his shoulder. He spun his head but saw nothing there.

"What the hell—"

No other words were forthcoming. Shadows crossed his face and something hard, vise-like, and freezing cold clamped over his mouth. His body rose from the ground.

Wendell screamed, but the icy darkness muffled him, forbidding even the slightest noise from escaping. The vise grew strong, crushing his face and biting into the flesh.

He struggled with all his might, clawing at whatever held him but only finding the bitter cold. It seeped into his skin like it was made of acid, cutting him like knives. He felt the pain even in the bones of his skull.

His scream was nothing, trapped in his mouth and his lungs as the cold forbade it from leaving. When death finally came, though after just mere seconds of agony, it was a relief.

Hartwell watched as the young man's body slumped and half fell to the ground. Lisette's dark shadow still held him by the face as she dragged him to the truck, pulling him inside with the other bodies.

He had nothing to say to her. She wouldn't listen even if he did. Instead, he watched the body slide back over the others and simply closed and latched the truck doors.

The carnival sounds followed him as he walked from the storage truck across the grounds. He stopped a couple of the rousties and other workers to let them know it was the carnival's last night in town. They'd head out at first light to somewhere new.

Reaching the far side of the midway, Hartwell entered the truck Artemis Bartolomy once called home, with its cramped little apartment in the back. He'd cleared out most of Bartolomy's trash. It was liveable now, homey even, if still too small for his liking.

Bart Hartwell sat at the tiny dining table and removed his hat before reaching for a bottle of bottom-shelf bourbon and a glass. He poured a double and stared at it for a long moment, the muffled sounds of the carnival music droning in his ears.

The room grew cold, and the shadows of Lisette manifested in the seat across from him. He didn't look up.

"You can't keep killing people," he said flatly. He had long lost any ability to drum up emotion when he spoke to her.

The ghost said nothing, as he knew she wouldn't.

"We need the workers. We can't run the carnival without workers. We'll have no one soon, and then what happens?"

The darkness shifted, and the shadows oozed closer like a silverfish creeping across the floor toward him. He stared at the bourbon and refused to look up. The cold crept over him and then her voice came, the quietest of whispers, in his ear. He listened because he had to, but his mind was focused on the bourbon. The curve of the glass, the color of the liquid, the distortion of the light through it. He focused as hard as he could as she whispered her poison into his soul.

CHAPTER 1

SO GOES DEATH

Shane Ryan sat across from the ghost of the Thousand Pound Man and sipped his coffee. Herbert had been a big fellow, to be sure, easily four hundred pounds, but he was not as big as all that. The carnival liked to exaggerate, especially where the so-called freaks were concerned. Anything to make them seem less human, or even monstrous.

Herbert assured Shane he had never felt bad about working under the name. He had made a lot of money, he had met a lot of friends, and there were plenty of benefits.

"You wouldn't believe how many women are interested in a giant man," Herbert said.

"I bet," Shane replied, hoping to avoid any details.

Shane and the big ghost had been on the road together since the death of Artemis Bartolomy. The carnival was gone, stolen by Bart Hartwell and the ghost called Lisette, and neither Shane nor Herbert had any idea what their plans were.

Lisette had taken her revenge on the people who were responsible for her boy's death some four decades in the past. But with that gone as a motive, there was no way to predict where they were taking the carnival or why.

"I'd kill for a turkey sandwich," Herbert said.

They were sharing a booth in a forgettable diner in upstate New York. Herbert's massive frame only fit in the seat because he was a ghost. It was strange to look at it, knowing he shouldn't have physically been able to wedge himself in the small space.

A server walked by holding a plate of fries and a sandwich. Shane asked for a coffee refill on her way back but didn't feel in the mood for a sandwich.

The police were after him for questioning. They would have certainly found his car and the corpses of Artemis Bartolomy and the judge Lisette took her vengeance upon in front of a burning, small-town courthouse.

Without Bart Hartwell on their radar, the only suspect the police had to link all the murders in the wake of the carnival's bloody trip through the northeast was Shane. And there would have been plenty of witnesses to the fire and dead bodies around his car.

Their luck in tracking Hartwell and Lisette had been non-existent. Once they discovered that the carnival was missing, there were no guesses or clues about where it was heading next. They were hoping for some new leads, though.

"This is our man," Herbert said suddenly. He was peering out the window to something beyond Shane. Shane said nothing and sipped his coffee.

Herbert made a habit of talking in public whenever the urge arose. Shane listened but rarely acknowledged, not wanting to draw attention to himself as the crazy man talking to an empty diner booth. Most people couldn't see Herbert, which was just as well. The ghost of a giant man would draw plenty of unwanted attention if seen.

A man in a hoodie walked past the diner outside and Herbert watched him intently. He entered and looked around until Shane made a quick gesture, indicating for him to come over.

The stranger was nervous, and his use of a hoodie and sunglasses made him look much shadier than he'd probably intended. He sat opposite Shane, nearly on top of Herbert, and leaned in. He shuddered at the sudden cold but quickly ignored it.

"Are you the guy?" he asked.

"Shane Ryan," Shane replied, taking another sip of his coffee.

"Cool, yeah. I'm Lowell."

"What have you got for me?" Shane asked. Lowell removed his sunglasses. He was younger than Shane expected, barely into his twenties.

"When Bart came back, a lot of the guys knew something was wrong," he explained, leaning over too far, and speaking too low. "Things got bad fast."

"How bad?"

Lowell looked around. It was clear he couldn't see Herbert.

"Lots of people walked. When he arrived, Bart acted like he was the boss. He told us he was running the show now, and that we should pack up, be ready to get on the road. Shiva stood up to him and told him no, that ain't happening."

"I take it didn't go over well?" Shane asked.

Lowell grimaced.

"Hell no, man. I saw a shadow come out of nowhere and pick her right up off the ground. A shadow! Killed her right there. I tell you, man, I ran. I don't know what happened next, who stayed, nothing. I bolted. I'm sure a lot of others did the same, but I have no idea who. I didn't wait to find out, that was it for me."

His voice rose as he spoke, getting overexcited, and Shane simply drank his coffee and waited until he finished.

"You don't know where they went after Bart took over?"

"No. I told you, I ran. I saw some weird stuff working for Mr. Bartolomy, but nothing like that. And I didn't want nothing to do with that guy. I think he killed Mr. Bartolomy."

"It was the shadow that killed Shiva, but yeah, you can say he was responsible," Shane confirmed.

Lowell hissed between clenched teeth and flopped back against the seatback, shaking his head.

"Do you know how long it took them to pack up?"

"No," Lowell said. "I went back later in the day. I thought maybe I could find Shiva, at least bury her, I don't know, but she was gone too. They must have taken her body. They abandoned some trucks; probably didn't have enough drivers, but that was it. I think they were going west, 'cuz where else can they go? Nothing going farther east, and we can't go into Canada."

"Right," Shane said.

The information was vague and didn't help at all. West was Shane's guess as well. That their numbers were diminished wasn't a great and helpful revelation, either. They were probably able to snag another hire or two in the next town and build their ranks that way. It was smarter to replace as many people as they could.

"So, are you planning on stopping Bart or something?" Lowell asked.

"If I can."

"I know you were friends with Bartolomy or something. I saw you hanging out the last few stops, but you gotta be careful, man. This is serious stuff. Bart had to be the guy killing all those people, using that shadow, and he's not done yet. I don't know how he's doing it, but he's dangerous."

"Yeah, seems like," Shane agreed.

Lowell had nothing else to offer about the carnival. It had taken them days to track down a former worker, and the information was all but useless. It took some effort not to swear.

Lowell slipped on his sunglasses once more and ducked out of the diner. Herbert sighed, shaking his big head.

"I knew this would be useless," he said.

"Maybe," Shane said softly into his mug. "We know they're short-staffed. And that Lisette is still looking for blood. That means the carnival won't be able to fade into the background. They're going to be trailing bodies again."

"But there weren't any," Herbert pointed out. "We didn't see Shiva or anyone in that empty lot. Or anywhere else. Lowell said the same thing about Shiva."

Shane nodded slightly, eyes searching the various diner patrons. Herbert was right again. They had not left bodies behind, which meant they were taking them for the ride, or hid them pretty well.

The bodies before had been left to jam up the carnival. Cops followed corpses, and the carnival had been implicated in a few murders. It had helped enough to let Lisette kill everyone she blamed for her son's death.

Now that Lisette and Hartwell were in charge of the carnival, they didn't want to be tracked. Keeping the bodies hidden benefited them in their bid to elude notice.

They might know Shane was after them, but neither of them really knew him. They had no reason to suspect he was more of a danger than anyone else. They were trying to evade notice from everyone.

They might have had a plan, and Shane needed more information if he hoped to sort it out. The carnival was the only home Lisette had ever known, so she wasn't looking to return to anything. The fact that they took the carnival at all implied they wanted to keep running it. That was baffling. Why?

"How are we going to find them?" Herbert asked, not for the first time.

The big ghost was antsy, not that Shane could blame him. But he was not good at dealing with it. Ghosts were, by nature, very stationary. Herbert had seen more of the world than most, on the road with the carnival for decades, but he was always rooted in the carnival. That had been taken from him in more ways than one, and he was singularly focused on getting back.

It was still not clear what he wanted to do if they found it. Even if Shane could destroy Lisette and they could take out Hartwell, then what? The carnival would never be what it was. He had not mentioned this to Herbert and didn't know if the ghost had considered what that meant, either.

If most of the old workers were gone, there might not even be anyone left who knew Herbert existed. There would be no one to keep his haunted item, no one to ensure he stayed with the carnival. He was going to have to adapt to a new way of life. Or death, to be more accurate.

"Don't you have any friends or contacts who can help us?" Herbert asked.

"I'm not a spy," Shane pointed out. "I don't have a network or whatever you think."

"Then what?"

"Then we plan. Cautious and smart. Montgomery was a bad situation, and I'm the prime murder suspect. That means you're either stuck pacing me in the shadows while we do this on the down-low, or I have to leave you somewhere. You want to haunt this diner forever?"

He spoke softly into his mostly empty coffee mug. Herbert grumbled, his expression one of frustration and anger, but he eventually nodded. He was a smart man, he was just shackled by circumstance. They both were.

Herbert had one potentially helpful idea. While Shane didn't have a team of agents ready to help him with fake IDs and untraceable cars to smuggle him across state lines, he had friends. Any bit of information he could glean about the carnival, or Hartwell and Lisette, could be helpful.

There were only so many ways a ghost could go on a killing spree before people took notice. If they had killed the carnival workers and taken the bodies on the road, things would eventually fall apart. They'd need to dump them somewhere or risk people noticing the smell. And that was a best-case scenario.

In the worst-case scenario, Lisette would be unable to restrain herself. Every place they stopped was a potential source of new victims. Hartwell had no control of her, all he could do was try to cover up her crimes. That sort of situation had a short shelf life. People would notice. The clock was ticking. What Shane needed was someone to keep an eye on that clock.

He set down his mug and pulled out his cell phone, staring at it for a long moment.

"You have someone to call?" Herbert asked with a tinge of hope.

"Maybe."

A sudden sense of unease came over him. The phone could be a liability. If the cops were building a case with him as a suspect, then they suspected that he'd killed multiple people in multiple states. That could have bumped the investigation up to something federal. They could be tracing his phone.

He got up from his seat and headed to a pay phone near the bathrooms, looking through his cell to find the number he needed before depositing a handful of quarters for the long-distance call.

The phone rang several times before someone picked up.

"Hello?" the familiar voice said.

"James, it's Shane. Can you talk?"

"You're going to want to make it a quick conversation, I should think," James Moran answered.

CHAPTER 2
THE SERIAL KILLER

"You getting some heat?" Shane asked.

"I've spoken with a gentleman from the FBI, if that's what you mean. He's very curious about what you've been doing the past few weeks."

Shane cursed in his head. The FBI made sense, though. They investigated serial murders.

"I explained that you're just a customer and I see you whenever you have an item of interest but that there's no formal business between us," James continued.

"They mentioned what they're looking into specifically?"

"Murder," James answered bluntly. "The agent—I can't recall his name—said you are wanted for questioning regarding a series of them. He was from something called the Behavioral Analysis Unit. Bit of an oddball."

That likely meant an APB had been put out on Shane. Certainly something beyond statewide. Might be a national one, which meant every cop between that diner and the Mexican and Canadian borders would have his picture at their fingertips. Hartwell and Lisette had jammed him up pretty well.

Going home was not an option; not that he really had planned on doing such a thing. They'd be sitting on his house in case he returned. He wished them well if they got a search warrant. That would probably go over poorly.

"Just to clarify, I didn't kill any of those people," Shane said.

"Of course," James agreed. "Didn't think you had."

"Glad to see you still have faith," Shane replied. He was going to see if James could help him track the carnival, but it was too much of a risk to get anyone else involved. For all he knew, the call was being monitored.

"Take care of yourself, James. I'll get in touch when this is cleared up."

"I expect a call soon, then. Be safe, Shane."

The phone line clicked, and Shane hung up. He and Herbert were on their own. Given the potential manhunt for Shane, the road ahead would not be easy. This was why he didn't like working with the living.

He returned to the booth and sat down. Herbert waited expectantly for news.

"Is everything okay?" the ghost asked.

"FBI thinks I'm a serial killer," he answered. "They're asking my known associates about me."

Herbert's expression dropped and Shane could see panic setting in.

"Doesn't change much," Shane said, trying to keep him calm.

"It doesn't? You're a wanted man."

"Same as before, just maybe a little more urgent and widespread. We'll manage. Find someplace off the radar for a while and maybe reach out to some people who don't know me that well who are plugged into this sort of thing."

"You're wanted for multiple murders," the ghost said louder this time. Shane shrugged and wondered where the server was. He badly needed that refill.

"Nothing I can do about that, Herbert. Unless you have some ideas."

"No," he admitted. "But I wouldn't be as calm about this if I were you."

"Sure you would," Shane responded. "You're a ghost. You'd be much calmer."

Herbert sighed dramatically and looked out the window while he regained his composure.

"Okay. We need a place to go that you have no ties to. Someplace we can still get help."

"Ideally," Shane said. Herbert turned to face him.

"I know a place. I haven't been there in forty years, but I know it's still around. They'll probably help."

Shane grinned. Herbert's tone lacked any conviction.

"You sure?" Shane asked.

"No. Not even a little bit. This person—this place—is from a long time ago. Friends once, I guess. But there was some bad blood with Artemis."

"Artemis is dead," Shane pointed out. Herbert frowned.

"I know," he replied quietly. Shane hadn't meant it to come off as insulting as Herbert seemed to take it.

"Is this an old business partner?"

"Sort of," the ghost admitted. "There's a town in Vermont, up near the Canadian border. It's a sort of retirement community for circus and carnival workers. Started back in the thirties with some freaks who wanted a place where they wouldn't be considered freaks anymore. Grew from that."

"And they chose northern Vermont?"

Herbert smiled and shrugged his big shoulders.

"They didn't like Florida, I guess."

Shane nodded. It sounded like their best bet. Old carnies might have the inside track on where Bartolomy and Sons was. Better odds than the average Joe, at least.

"The people there are not always open to outsiders. Most of the residents know someone who knows someone, if you follow me."

"I know you," Shane pointed out. Herbert grunted.

"Yes, sir, you do. But I'm a ghost, as you've noted. Not everyone in town will see me. Mr. Rags can see ghosts though, and that's all that matters. But last I heard, more than a thousand people lived in Roland

Hills. It could get awkward if you're there asking about carnies and murder. Folks might think you're the law, and carnies aren't traditionally fans of the law."

"Well, neither am I. We'll get along like gangbusters, I'm sure."

Herbert sighed again and nodded.

"We're going to need a car."

Shane didn't think they were at the grand theft auto portion of their journey just yet. No need to draw any more attention than necessary. Instead, he nodded at the window, focused on a building about a block away on the far side of the street.

Herbert turned in his seat and looked out.

"Bus station?" he said.

"We're traveling in style," Shane confirmed. Just as long as no one had sent his picture to the bus stations yet, it would be one of the most inconspicuous ways to get where they were going.

They left the diner, Shane pulling up his hood to be less noticeable. The bus station was small and desolate, and if they'd sent out Shane's picture already, the girl working the ticket booth had not bothered to look at it. She barely looked at Shane.

He bought a ticket to Newport, Vermont, which Herbert said was as close as they were going to get to their destination, and then they sat on a bench and waited for an hour and twenty minutes in almost complete silence.

Shane didn't want to talk, and it seemed Herbert wasn't too keen on it, either. Only one other person came into the bus station as they sat, a middle-aged lady with frizzy hair who scowled at Shane for no reason and then sat on the opposite side of the room reading a beat-up paperback novel.

Herbert sat in the seat opposite Shane once the bus arrived. The vehicle looked like a relic of the eighties, and the upholstery might have been from a few decades before that. It was half-full of passengers, none of whom looked happy. Few even looked up when Shane boarded, which suited him fine. No one wanted to acknowledge anyone else on a bus, it seemed.

By the time they passed the border into Vermont, Herbert was back to chatting again, explaining the history of Roland Hills in much greater detail than Shane had ever wanted to hear.

Two hours on the bus felt like six, but they finally arrived in Newport in the middle of the afternoon. Shane was glad to be free of the vehicle and out of the dank, poorly lit space. Their chances of freely traveling like that would be limited soon enough. In a bigger city, they would likely be more on the ball about watching out for potential serial killers. He hoped Herbert's idea would pay off.

Hitching a ride to Roland Hills was more of a challenge. The town was about an hour away according to Herbert, and Shane was not the sort of man who comforted drivers who might have considered picking up a hitcher. He and Herbert walked about seven miles before a trucker pulled over and picked them up.

"Not a lot of folks heading to Roland Hills these days," the trucker said with a chuckle when Shane said where he was going.

"Just looking up an old friend," he replied.

The trucker's name was Eddie. He was missing a few teeth and probably could have used a haircut during the last Presidential administration, but he was friendly enough.

"Ah, so you know what it's like, then. With the circus folk."

"Yeah," Shane said. Herbert was half-in and half-out of the truck cab with them, listening quietly as the trucker shared some of his experiences.

"I do a run between Manchester and Trois-Rivières twice a month, so I stop into Roland Hills now and then. Found it by accident a few years back, to be honest. Pileup on the highway had me detour, found Roland Hills, stopped at this diner for lunch, and loved it. Little folks run it. Fella called himself Tom Thumb back in the day. Got some amazing stories," Eddie explained.

Herbert laughed in the back.

"Old Tom is still alive? He was a cad, that one. Two feet tall and as lecherous as any man I ever met."

"You know the place?" Eddie asked.

"Never been. Heard some stories about Mr. Thumb, though."

Eddie chuckled.

"I bet you have. They're good people. Got a raw deal from the world, though. People calling them freaks and whatnot. No different than being born with red hair or a birthmark, if you ask me."

"Everyone has their story, that's for sure," Shane agreed.

"I know they get a little persnickety with outsiders, partly why I don't stop there so often these days. Things were good for a spell. Town was up to maybe five thousand and growing, then it hit a downswing. Lots of bad blood there."

"Bad blood?" Shane asked. Eddie nodded.

"Oh yeah. People moving in to start businesses and maybe not appreciating the town's history? That's what I gathered. Anyway, town shrank again. Mostly original residents now; lots of empty houses and shops. Tough times for everyone these days."

"Tougher for some."

"Preaching to the choir, my friend," Eddie said. "I gotta pick up two or three more hauls a month just to make ends meet these days."

"When were you last in Roland Hills?" Shane asked, trying to stay on topic.

"Oh, hmm. Must have been a year now. Just after those boys died in the barn fire. Things were tense, if you follow me. Got the feeling folks didn't want me around. Not me specifically, mind you. Just anyone. That's why I was surprised you wanted to go there."

"Yeah," Shane said, not quite sure what Eddie meant but gleaning enough to know they might be walking into a whole new problem. "Just looking for an old friend. I think I'll be fine."

"For sure, for sure," Eddie said.

The truck driver was correct that the town was by no means on a main road. It was barely on a side road. They had to exit I-91 and head down progressively smaller and smaller routes until they were on what looked like a single-lane dirt road through the woods alongside a small river.

"How did you ever find this place, Eddie?" Shane asked, watching the endless forest roll past. The trucker smiled sheepishly.

"I maybe heard rumors here and there. I loved the carnival when I was a kid, got word some folks retired out here. It was sort of on my route, so I figured why not? Glad I did."

"Makes two of us," Shane agreed. Having to hunt it down himself would have taken more time than he would have wanted to put into it.

"Here we are," Eddie said as the trees thinned out and they passed a ramshackle sign that read "Roland Hills".

The truck rumbled past some open fields and then a lot with a small farmhouse set back well away from the street. Soon, more buildings appeared, closer together until they were in what looked like a bit of a sprawl. The mixture of structures was perplexing; none of them were built according to any recognizable architectural style Shane could think of. Many appeared to be built from scratch out of timber, aluminum, and sometimes brick, but with all kinds of add-ons made from different materials, like an advanced shantytown. Some appeared abandoned, and others were burned out.

By the time they reached what should have been downtown, with brick buildings that looked to be from the twenties at the latest, the modest-sized town had proven to be unlike anything Shane had seen. It was like a pile of leftovers thrown together with no rhyme or reason.

Eddie pulled to a stop outside of Tom Thumb's diner. The buildings on either side were abandoned, but the diner looked to be doing brisk business, with a handful of patrons inside.

"This work for you?" Eddie asked.

"Yeah, it's great. Thank you," Shane said. Eddie nodded as Shane climbed down from the cab. When the truck was on its way again, Shane looked at Herbert.

"Where to?" he asked.

"Rags lives up that way," the ghost said, pointing ahead. He looked around nervously, noticing the faces in windows that looked out at Shane.

"We should go quickly."

Shane looked around at the same unfriendly faces.

"Yeah," he said. "Let's do that."

CHAPTER 3

THE WEREWOLF

No one disturbed them on their walk to Mr. Rags' house. Some residents gave Shane a dirty look in passing, but it wasn't as bad as he and Herbert had feared. If the worst thing he had to deal with was dirty looks, he'd be okay.

Rags' home was an old farmhouse at the end of a side road. The property was vast and unused from what Shane could see. Overgrown fields of weeds and wildflowers gave way to forest and part of the river far in the back. A half-collapsed barn sat a good trek from the main house, and a couple of sheds lay in equal states of disrepair. The large lawn was sprinkled with at least a dozen run-down, rusted-out cars and trucks.

Rags lived far enough from downtown that he was isolated on his land, with his nearest neighbor so far down the road that the house was barely noticeable from the lawn.

"Mr. Rags was a big act in his day," Herbert explained as they approached. "He was never with Bartolomy as a freak. He was more of… I'm not sure what you'd call him. A consultant? He helped Bartolomy Sr. spruce things up back before what happened with Lisette and Dash. Back when things were still good."

"He's a freakshow expert?" Shane asked.

"Oh, definitely. He's got hypertrichosis. Gave him a unique insight," the ghost said.

"I'm not sure what that means."

Herbert looked at him as they walked up the overgrown driveway.

"It's almost the opposite of you, I suppose."

That description was even less helpful, but Shane didn't press the matter. They had reached the farmhouse, a three-story yellow brick building that looked like it was on its last legs. Some of the brickwork on the chimney had already crumbled, and the outside shutters were more peeled paint than not. Everything looked tired and old.

The warped wooden steps of the porch creaked under Shane's weight, and he hoped the whole thing wasn't about to collapse. He pulled open an old aluminum screen door that screeched and whined on rusty hinges before he knocked on a thick wooden door that was once sky blue but now was faded and chipped after years of neglect.

"You sure he still lives here?" Shane asked.

"No," Herbert admitted. "But where else would he be?"

Shane grunted in response.

Something thudded and creaked inside. Shane waited and heard more creaking and then footsteps before the door lock turned. The hinges squealed, and the door opened slightly.

A fur-covered face stared out through the crack, blue eyes narrow and fixed on Shane.

"Who the hell are you?"

"Shane Ryan," he answered.

Though he was mostly obscured by the door, it was clear that the man talking to Shane was covered in a thick coating of dark hair. Not an inch of bare flesh was visible.

"Good for you," the furry man said. He closed the door, and the lock clicked.

"Rags! Rags, it's Herbert," the ghost yelled through the door. He could have just walked into the house if he wanted, but Shane didn't think Herbert had spent a lot of time acting like a true ghost in his afterlife.

The lock clicked again. Mr. Rags' face appeared once more. Herbert came closer, and Shane backed up to allow him some room.

"Herbert? Jesus H. Christ, what the hell happened to you?"

He let the door fall open and Shane could see now that Rags' entire body was covered in hair. He wore a tank top and boxer shorts, but his arms and legs and even his hands were covered. Ironically, his chest looked to have the thinnest hair, enough that the flesh could at least be seen beneath it, but the hair on his face and arms was as dense as the hair on his head.

"I died," Herbert answered.

"Good gravy, big man, did you ever. Oh my stars, when? What happened?"

"Long time ago." Herbert shrugged. "Heart gave out."

Rags shook his head.

"'Course it did. What did I tell you, man? You can't sit on your behind eating yourself to death."

"I know," Herbert said, smiling. "You look good."

"I look like hell," Rags countered. "Losing the hair on my chest. Who the hell goes chest bald? I'm going to look like this fella soon enough."

He pointed to Shane and sneered, and Herbert laughed.

"This is Shane," Herbert said.

"I heard him the first time. The hell you two here for?"

"You must have been a real hit in the carnival back in the day," Shane pointed out. Rags fixed him with a glare. He was several inches shorter than Shane, and beneath the furry frame, he looked extremely thin and frail.

"Oh, you brought a comedian. Are you going to tell me to look on the bright side of life? All the memories of the joy I brought to little girls and boys who pulled my hair and called me a monster for thirty-odd years? I'll stick my hairy foot up your backside and we'll see who's a real hit."

Shane had to laugh, which seemed to make Rags even angrier. Herbert forced himself between them.

"We need help, Rags. This is serious. Something bad has happened."

The words hung in the air, and Rags finally grumbled, backing away from the door.

"Alright, alright. Come on in. Excuse the mess; the maid hasn't been here since the seventies."

He led them down a dusty hall with corners caked with cobwebs, and into a living room strewn with trash. There were random food wrappers and cans and bags and boxes tossed about haphazardly. Rags had a spot clear, with a chair facing an old TV set in a wooden cabinet, but the rest of the room was an "every man for himself" situation. There was a sofa, but it was buried in crushed beer cans, cracker boxes, and wrappers from beef jerky and potato chips.

Herbert took it all in, immersed up to his shins in junk, while Shane had to kick soup cans and half-filled trash bags out of his way to find flat floor on which to stand.

"Rags, what happened?" Herbert asked sadly.

"You tell me. You said something bad."

"No, what happened here? Your place?"

The hairy man shrugged, his attention now split between his guests and a game show on TV.

"The mess, you mean?"

"Yes, the mess. This isn't safe. Or healthy," Herbert said.

"You ate yourself to death; don't tell me what's healthy," Rags grumbled.

"You know what I mean."

"Yeah. Sure thing, big man. It's just... who cares, right?"

"People care. What happened to Treble? Or Martin?"

"Deader than you," Rags answered. "It's been a long time, Herbert."

"But—"

"Nothing to but about," Rags interrupted. "I'm in my eighties. I've lived longer than I expected. Now, you got some stuff to tell me or not?"

Herbert nodded, trying to ignore the mess.

"Artemis is dead. Linskey is gone, too. And Shiva."

"Sheesh. Over time, or do you mean all of 'em together?"

"Basically together. Lisette's gone mad. She's been killing the people she blamed for her boy dying."

"That business," Rags said. "I heard about that back when. That was ages ago, though."

"She was trapped for a long time. One of our roustabouts, Bart Hartwell, freed her. He'd been in love with her forever. They went on a killing spree, only it got even more out of hand. They have control of the carnival after they killed off anyone in their way. I don't know what the plan is, but she'll murder anyone who crosses her."

Rags let out a dramatic exhale and leaned back in his chair.

"Jesus, big man. You tell me you got bad news, you mean it. What are we talking about here? How many dead?"

"Probably dozens now, I think," Herbert said.

Rags cursed, now just staring wide-eyed.

"And they killed Arty?"

"Yeah…" Herbert sighed. "Lisette is… I don't know, Rags. She's rage. She's just hate, and no one can stop her. Except him," the ghost replied, indicating Shane.

"What's so special about the chrome dome?"

"I can stop her," Shane answered. Rags scoffed.

"So big man says. This is a ghost we're talking about, right? Lisette from back in the day?"

"The same," Herbert said. "Shane can… hurt us. Ghosts, I mean."

Rags' eyes narrowed again.

"That a fact? Never heard of that trick."

"Not a trick, just a thing I can do. We need to stop her, though. She's beyond vengeance. Any innocent person who stumbles into the carnival could set her off; there's no way to know."

"And you thought of me because…?" Rags asked Herbert.

"My hands are tied, being dead and all," the ghost admitted. "And

Lisette's murders were pinned on Shane."

"Good gravy, man," Rags said, shaking his head again. "A dead man and a wanted killer, and you're trying to hunt down a murder sideshow with the help of a retired dog boy? You're gonna need to pray for a miracle."

"You know people, Rags. I know you do. Contacts who might have at least heard of where the carnival is. Give us a place to look for them."

Rags growled, befitting his appearance.

"It's going to take some time. I have to make some calls, probably leave messages and wait to hear back. You have any idea where I should start looking?"

"Last place we know of them is New York. Probably went west, but we don't have anything else to go on."

"Better make yourselves comfortable, then. Gotta find my phone. And my phone book. And maybe a magic wand."

He began rooting around on a side table, tossing trash from a drawer. Shane looked at Herbert, who shrugged apologetically.

"We're not as in the loop around here as we once were," Rags said, rifling through the pages of a small notebook. "Each year takes a toll. Most folks in town aren't even carnies anymore. Just a random lot of misfits these days, folks who want to live off the grid and away from prying eyes, if you follow."

"No police?" Shane asked. Rags chuckled.

"I don't know if you noticed, but this is a town in the sense that there are buildings assembled in a small space. The real town of Roland Hills vanished years ago. Then circus folk moved in, expanded, renovated, and built a new life. This town isn't on any maps. We don't have a post office, no courthouse, no cops. We're our own thing out here. So I can help you maybe, but it'll take a bit."

Shane wasn't put off by Rags' demeanor, and he also didn't expect a miracle. Tracking down a carnival that didn't want to be found would take time, and he wasn't surprised by any of it. But he didn't want to wait out the process in Rags' scrapyard of a house, either.

He and Herbert had been lying low for a while now and he hadn't had much time to himself to just think. Roland Hills seemed like the dark side of the moon, and if there was any place he could get a few moments to himself with little fear of the FBI rolling up on him, it was that place.

"I'm going to head out for a bit, get some air," Shane said.

Rags grumbled, looking up from his notebook.

"You saying my place stinks?" he asked. Shane nodded.

"It does."

"Smartass. Wouldn't head into town if I was you. Folks don't take kindly to newcomers."

"So I've heard. I'll be unobtrusive," he replied. The old carny ignored him, going back to his books. Herbert looked concerned.

"Is everything alright?" he asked. Shane chuckled.

"Not even remotely, but I'm just going to stretch my legs. Stay here and catch up with your friend. Come get me if you hear anything before I return."

"Watch your back," Herbert advised.

"Always," Shane said, heading out the creaky front door. The porch moaned under his weight again, the sort of stressed and ominous sound he expected to hear in a forgotten, haunted building. In a way, he supposed Rags' house was haunted, just by someone who wasn't dead yet.

He headed back down the path to the road, wishing he had some more insight into where he was going to go next.

CHAPTER 4
THE DEVIL

If Roland Hills was full of circus people, others might know how to track down a carnival. Even if many of them had passed on like Rags said, some had to be around. Fond of outsiders or not, Shane was certain he could be of more use outside of the hairy man's house than trapped inside while he made phone calls.

He took a left away from Rags' property. The closest neighbor that way was another farmhouse and seemed like the sort of place another old-timer like Rags might call home. Worst-case scenario, it was someone who knew nothing. At least Shane would have time to stretch his legs.

No cars passed, not that he expected any to, and there was no sign of life on his walk. The neighboring farmhouse was inexplicably worse off than Rags'. The roof had caved in sometime in the not-so-recent past, and plants were growing in the exposed guts of the house, including a couple of trees that were at least a few years old.

A weather-beaten old barn stood beyond the house, a few panels missing in the frame. From the road, Shane caught a quick flash of movement in the barn, something moving between the missing wall slats. There was no way anything living could call the house a home, but the barn was another matter.

He trudged up a driveway overgrown with weeds and then waded through a sea of much more robust plant life once he passed the broken house into the field beyond. The grass was waist-high in places, and some weeds grew as tall as Shane, covered in thorny leaves and big, purple flowers.

As he got closer to the barn, the weeds thinned out some. The growth pattern was patchier, and those that grew were shorter and less vibrant. A familiar feeling came over him. Living things had a hard time growing near the barn. He knew what that meant.

There was no sound from inside the building and when he approached, there was no longer any obvious movement. The big barn doors were chained ineffectively. The rusty length of metal was almost brown with age and had been set so loosely that one door hung open with enough space for someone of even Herbert's size to enter without difficulty.

Light came in through the many cracks and missing planks in the barn board, but the interior was still a patchwork of light and shadow. Shane ducked under the rusted chain and entered the barn, breathing in the warm, still air that smelled like mulch and rotten wood and dust.

There was no farm equipment inside the building, just piles of chopped wood and trash. An old mattress that probably hadn't been used in a decade was covered in black and green mold, and faded cans were piled all around it.

Shane couldn't see anyone, but the air had a chill to it that made him certain he was not alone. He stood in the doorway, scanning the barn's interior.

"Sorry to interrupt you if you're busy here. Just need to ask you a few questions," he said. There was no movement and no reply. Ghosts were often pretty eager to chat someone up, and from the looks of things, no one had visited the barn in ages.

"Probably not too up-to-date on current events in here though, are you?"

A shape drifted from the shadows in the farthest corner of the barn. Shane watched it, waiting for it to get closer. Even when the figure moved toward the light, it took him longer than he'd expected to puzzle out what he was seeing.

The ghost was of a man, his features mostly hidden by dark, tribal tattoos. His face was overlaid with a mask tattoo that appeared to be Polynesian in design, like a demon but highly stylized. More curious was the top of the ghost's bald head, where an actual horn grew off-centered above his left eye. It rose straight up and came to a point at the end, like a unicorn's, or some demon from a horror movie. It reminded Shane of Diablo, only his horns had been implanted surgically and this one appeared to be real.

"You wouldn't happen to know a guy named Diablo, would you?" Shane asked.

The ghost stopped moving, but it was hard to say if it was the question that stopped him or that Shane had acknowledged him.

"Papa Diablo," the ghost said in a gravelly voice with a Creole accent. "They call me Papa Diablo."

"Oh. I recently met another Diablo. His horns were a little different, though."

Papa Diablo smiled, his body half hunched over. His teeth were silver, not a single real one in his mouth, and the effect was even more off-putting than the horn.

"My little man, Diablo. Sure, yeah, I know that one. Where he at?"

"Not sure," Shane admitted. "Maybe in jail. Got mixed up in some ugliness."

"Jail, sure. He a hothead," Papa Diablo said.

"So… you're his father?"

"Baaaahhh," Papa Diablo grumbled, making a face. "No boy of mine. He a student. I mentor him long time back. Give him his first tattoo. How you know Diablo?"

The ghost came closer, still bent and walking like he was doing a bit, performing a creepy walk for a crowd rather than just having a barn chat with a stranger.

"Bartolomy and Sons," Shane answered. "Got into some bad stuff together."

"What that mean? Bad stuff? What bad stuff?"

The closer he got, the more convinced Shane was that the man's horn was a real thing, or had been when he was alive. It had the look of a thick, gnarly fingernail, dark brown and black but yellow where it grew thinner.

"There was a ghost at the carnival that started killing people. Diablo got picked up by the police as a suspect."

"What ghost?" Papa Diablo asked suspiciously. In the light, Shane could now see the spirit was entirely nude and covered in as many tattoos as Diablo had been, though everything on Papa Diablo was thick, black, and tribal. His body was rail-thin beneath, enough that his ribs and hip bones protruded.

"Her name was Lisette," Shane answered.

Papa Diablo's eyes lit up, and he grimaced.

"Burkitt. That boy that get killed there," he said.

"Right," Shane confirmed. "She got loose. Got revenge on the people from Burkitt."

"She went back? Went to Burkitt?"

"No, she—" Shane began, but Papa Diablo hissed and scuttled closer, raising a single, tattooed finger in his face.

"You don't go there. She there, you leave it, hear me? You don't go there."

"You've been to Burkitt?" Shane asked.

"That Burkitt, that a cursed town. Evil town. You best leave her if that where she went."

It was not often that a ghost expressed fear, but Shane had seen it from time to time. A holdover from life, something that had been so terrifying that even death couldn't shake it. Having been to Burkitt, Shane could only imagine what Papa Diablo might have experienced there.

"What happened there?" he asked.

Papa Diablo might have been with Bartolomy and Sons back in the day, but they had never been in Burkitt proper, as far as Shane knew. Papa Diablo would have had to go into town on his own, or through some other means at some other time.

"Death happen. That town belong to him."

"To Death?" Shane asked. Papa Diablo nodded.

"You see this?" he asked, touching the horn on his head as if Shane could have missed it. "Doctor call it cutaneous horn. Just a… thing. A growth. But I use it, yeah? I play the Devil in my act; I scare the folks. This Burkitt? That where the real Devil live. You don't go there."

He scuttled back from Shane, his movements a jarring mixture of abrupt, jerking motions and fluid, dance-like ones. Shane was sure his act was something to behold back in the day.

"I'm just looking for the carnival. I don't think they went to Burkitt. But they killed people. Artemis Bartolomy and others," Shane explained.

Papa Diablo hissed and shook his head.

"Artemis. Good man, he was. Good man. Good to me and mine. He deserve better."

"Lisette has the carnival now. She's taken it, and we don't know where they went."

Papa Diablo scowled and shook his head.

"I don't know about them now. This my home here. Alone in here. This is best for me."

"Yeah," Shane said, looking around the barn. It looked like the end of life had not been entirely kind to Papa Diablo, but he was alone now and far removed from whatever had happened. Far removed from the world.

"Remember what I say," Papa Diablo said. "You stay away from that place."

"What did you see in Burkitt?" Shane asked. Lisette was his pressing concern, finding the carnival, and Hartwell, and a way to clear his name. But at the center of everything was Burkitt. Something in that town had set everything in motion. Shane didn't think it was Death or the Devil, but he had no doubt there was darkness there.

"Told you what I saw there. Death. The Devil. Darkness made real. Just stay away."

Shane could only nod. The ghost probably did not know what he'd seen. The dead in Burkitt were twisted things, some of them more monster than human. Barely recognizable.

If there was something more in Burkitt, something that got the ball rolling on the town's path toward death and destruction, it could have been much darker and more powerful than what he'd experienced.

The dead in Burkitt had not died of natural causes. The boys Lisette's son tried to save were killed by a twisted entity, and maybe it was the devil Papa Diablo spoke of, or maybe it was just another deranged spirit that Burkitt had produced.

There was a reason to go to Burkitt, no matter what Papa Diablo said, but Shane would have to put it on the back burner for now. The darkness there could be cleaned up later.

"I'll keep my distance," Shane assured the ghost.

Papa Diablo's dark smile reappeared and he cocked his head, eyeing Shane with suspicion.

"No," he said, "you won't. But Papa Diablo can't stop that. You been warned. Wash my hands of it."

He wiped his palms against one another in a dismissive gesture and crouched in the shadows.

"Guess I'll be on my way, then. Thanks for the chat," Shane said.

"You tell Diablo come visit me. Tell him he owe me that," the ghost said. Shane nodded and made his way back out of the door and into the field.

There was more going on behind the scenes of carnival life than he ever would have imagined. He wished it was easier to piece it together, to track them down and finish what he needed, but tracking ghosts was rarely a straightforward task. Especially ones that were so mobile and had help from the living.

He wasn't ready to head back to Rags' home yet, but he wasn't sure he wanted to get to know anyone else in Roland Hills, either. Maybe heeding the warnings about avoiding people there would be best.

Shane had been letting Burkitt simmer in the back of his mind since his visit to the town. He was almost positive it was not related to Lisette. It had helped create her, but not directly, and he was sure she had no reason to go back there.

Still, he could not shake the feeling that once everything else with Bartolomy and Sons was taken care of, things would not be truly over until he returned to Burkitt and faced the Devil.

CHAPTER 5

THE UNWANTED

It was nearly evening when Shane returned to Rags' home to see if any progress had been made. He was surprised to see that the house had been seriously overhauled in his absence, with much of the trash gone and the living spaces cleared.

"What happened in here?" Shane asked, entering the living room. Herbert was on the couch, but Rags was nowhere to be seen. Elsewhere in the house, thumps and bangs echoed through the walls.

"Rags made some calls, and we're waiting for callbacks once some friends look into the carnival. A friend of his came over and lit into him for having company in what she called a pig sty. She's forcing him to help her clean up."

Trash fell like rain past a window and Shane peered out, seeing junk piled outside. More was tossed from above, followed by a woman cursing.

"He has friends?" Shane asked.

"Her name is Giselle. She was a bearded lady in the same sideshow as Rags."

"Of course," Shane said.

"They're getting a room ready for you. We're probably going to have to spend the night."

Shane sighed. He was not eager to spend the night in whatever version of a clean room Rags could provide, but he'd probably slept in worse places. It'd be nice to stay in a place where he could relax and not have to worry about the cops finding him.

"Find anything on your walk?"

"Nothing helpful," Shane said. He made a mental note to mention the ghost to Diablo if he saw him again, but otherwise, there was little help in what the spirit had said.

More thumping from upstairs and some muffled cursing drew his attention. If he had to spend the night there, he could at least handle prepping his room. It wasn't like they were at a hotel, and he didn't need to give Rags another excuse to be surly.

Herbert followed Shane upstairs to a bedroom that looked like no one had slept in it since the house was built. Giselle, to Shane's surprise, was not a woman with a beard. She might have once been, but now she looked like anyone's grandma, a woman of average height and build with white hair in a bun and no hair on her face.

She tossed a handful of old bottles out the window as Shane entered, proving her housekeeping skills were perhaps a little rusty, and looked him up and down.

"You gotta be the house guest," she said, her voice husky. Sweat was beading on her brow, and she wore a pair of yellow rubber gloves. Rags turned and looked at him, then grunted.

"Yeah, that's the one," he confirmed.

"She can't see me," Herbert pointed out to Shane.

"Can't imagine what you want with this fuzzy old cuss, but I gotta say, I'm not disappointed to see you," Giselle said, smiling at him. Shane raised an eyebrow.

"Lord, woman, you're old enough to be his mother," Rags said.

"But I'm not his momma, am I?" she replied.

"I can finish up in here. It's fine. Really," Shane said. Giselle walked over to him and put a gloved hand on his chest.

"Nonsense. I've been trying to force this man to clean his house for fifteen years. He's earned this. Go find yourself something to drink in the kitchen. Lord knows he's got enough beer to float a ship. I'm gonna make sure you're nice and comfy."

"I'd go if I were you," Rags said. "Stay here, and she'll be flirting enough to make you blush. No shame."

"Shame's for the boring. You're not boring are you, Mr....?"

"Call me Shane," he answered. "Not sure if I'm boring, but I might not be exciting enough for you."

Giselle laughed, a little more dramatically than she needed to.

"Oh, I bet you're just a delight," she said.

"Think I'll go find a beer, maybe see some more sights since we have time."

"Don't wander too far," Giselle suggested.

Shane nodded and excused himself, taking Herbert back downstairs with him. Roland Hills was proving to be a much stranger destination than he had expected.

He sat in the kitchen, which was more cluttered than messy, and drank one of Rags' beers while the ghost sat opposite him on the tiniest of kitchen chairs.

"We don't have to go anywhere," Herbert said. "I know Rags is difficult, but he was on top of everything. People in the business respect him. If anyone knows anything, we'll hear soon enough."

"I know," Shane said. "Not worried about that, I just don't like doing nothing."

"Not much we can do."

Shane finished the beer and looked out the kitchen window. The sun was setting, and the sky was gray. He wanted to see more of the town, see if there were more like Papa Diablo. He couldn't learn much about Lisette in town, but if Papa Diablo had known about Burkitt, maybe some others did, too.

"Let's go look around town," Shane said to Herbert, getting up from the table.

"You heard what Eddie said. And Rags," the ghost pointed out.

"Yeah. I'm sure we can take care of ourselves."

"I can. I don't know about you though," Herbert said. Shane laughed and headed out with the ghost on his heels.

They walked down the road they had traveled to get to Rags' home, this time heading back into the oldest part of town where Eddie had dropped them off. It was asking for trouble, as Herbert had pointed out, but that was half the point. Maybe they'd stir up something useful.

"How many people in town used to be part of Bartolomy and Sons?" Shane asked as they walked. The sky had faded to a mosaic of orange and purple and blue as the sun cast its last rays from the west. A handful of others were out walking as well, including what looked to Shane to be a three-legged man with his dog.

"The carnival has been around for a long while. Lots of people passed through over the years. Maybe a dozen freaks retired here. Handful of rousties, too."

"We don't want to talk to any of them?" Shane asked. Herbert laughed nervously.

"Some are dead now. Others didn't leave on the best terms. Artemis was a good guy, but if there was a dispute over money, he could get... combative."

"Sure," Shane said. "How many folks in town know about Burkitt?"

The ghost gave him a sidelong glance as they approached the town's main street.

"About what happened to Dash?" he asked.

"No. The town of Burkitt. How many of the people here know about the town?"

"I'm not sure I follow," Herbert admitted.

Shane pulled a cigarette from the pack in his pocket and paused on the street corner to light it. More people were on the street now, and not all of them were alive. A pair of ghosts walked the sidewalks a block to the west, not together. He turned toward them.

"I met Papa Diablo earlier, you know him?"

Herbert's eyes lit up.

"Papa D? Of course! He was with us way back. I had no idea he's still alive. He must be over a hundred years old by now."

"He's not. Alive, I mean," Shane told him. "He's Rags' neighbor. Haunts the barn."

Herbert turned and looked back the way they'd come.

"He's there? We should go back. I haven't seen him—"

"He told me the devil lives in Burkitt," Shane said, cutting him off. He took a long drag from the cigarette as he walked, forcing Herbert to keep up with him instead of going back.

"What's that supposed to mean?" he asked.

Shane shook his head, keeping his eyes on the ghosts in front of them.

"No idea. But I saw a lot of ghosts in Burkitt, too. Your friend Papa D told me that if Lisette went there, under no circumstances should we follow. What happened to Dash, to Lisette, and this whole mess we're a part of, started because of something wrong in the town that no one knows anything about. Got me curious about what's so special about it. What happened in Burkitt?"

Herbert had nothing to say for a long moment while they walked. He could only shake his head.

"I don't know, Shane. We never even went into the town. We were outside the whole time. Some of the living went there, but they didn't warn us of anything. We never would have stayed if we knew the danger; you have to believe that."

"I do," Shane assured him. "I'm not saying you're keeping secrets, Herbert, don't get me wrong. I just get the feeling we're missing the forest for the trees, you know?"

"I'm not sure. There was obviously that thing in Burkitt, that horrible thing that killed the boys, but what are you suggesting?"

"Not sure," Shane admitted. "You've seen that there's more than one kind of ghost out there. You seem like you're not much different now than you were in life. But the thing that killed those boys, and the thing Lisette became... that's what happens to some spirits. Sometimes, they're even worse."

"How could anything be worse?" Herbert asked softly.

"You don't want to know. But it happens."

He exhaled a cloud of smoke and crossed the street, heading toward the nearest ghost. The spirit was a woman who was almost impossibly tall, well over seven feet, with long, matted hair and a deep, angry bruise around her neck.

"Oh! I know her! They called her Queen Priscilla," Herbert said as he recognized the dead woman. "Tallest woman in the world."

"I'd buy that," Shane said.

"Hello, Ms. Priscilla," Herbert called out before they reached her. The ghost turned, her white, dead eyes focused on them.

"I don't know you," she said flatly.

"It's me, Herbert. From Bartolomy and Sons. We met back—"

"I don't know you," she said again, turning her back on them.

Herbert frowned and looked ready to call out to her again until Shane put a hand on the ghost's shoulder. The cold ran up his arm, but he squeezed the big man firmly.

"Like I said. Not everyone comes back like they were."

They passed the giant spirit and continued to the end of the next block. The Roland Hills Cemetery awaited them there, an informal little patch of land behind a shin-high stone wall and bedecked with randomly placed headstones of all shapes and sizes.

The spirits of freaks and seemingly normal-looking people roamed the darkness. Their numbers were not staggering, but Shane could see at least a dozen from the sidewalk.

"Any familiar faces?" Shane asked. Herbert shook his head.

"Not really. Judging by the clothes, I think a lot of them are before my time."

He was right. Several ghosts looked like they might have been from nearly a hundred years in the past. If they were dead before Herbert or Lisette's time, they'd provide little information of value.

Shane finished his cigarette, intent on returning to Rags' house, when one of the spirits in the cemetery made a beeline toward them, scampering among the tombstones.

"What is that?" Herbert asked. Shane raised an eyebrow.

"You're asking me?"

The spirit was obviously human, it had to be, but it was not something Shane had ever seen. The ghost's face looked like it was covered in jagged bits of bark that grew from his cheeks, eyebrows, and forehead. The body was covered in more of the same, especially the hands and feet, which looked like enormous, gnarled piles of twisted roots. It looked like a tree that had come to life.

"You don't belong here," the tree ghost bellowed.

"Tree Man," Herbert said, his voice a shocked whisper.

"What the hell is a Tree Man?" Shane asked.

"It's a disease, like Alligator Boy or Lobster Man. Produces these growths, but this is so much more advanced than when I saw him last."

Tree Man stomped toward them on his root-like feet and swung a massive stump of a hand in their direction. The attack was clumsy, and Shane ducked back and out of the way, but Herbert was not expecting the assault and took the brunt of the swing on the side of his face.

Herbert collapsed to one side, ignored by Tree Man, who continued toward Shane.

"You don't belong here!"

CHAPTER 6

TREE MAN

Shane grunted as the ghost's gnarled fist slammed into his gut. He'd been punched enough times to know how to take a hit, but he'd never been hit by anyone with a fist the size of a basketball covered in jagged edges and knobs.

"We're just passing through," Shane explained, backing away from another swing. Tree Man was angry. When he made contact, it was powerful, but he was also clumsy. Shane guessed he had never been a fighter, and he didn't have a very refined technique.

"Go," the angry spirit growled.

"Happily," Shane replied. The ghost swung again, forcing Shane to dodge to one side, ducking to his knees.

Tree Man raised a club-like hand again and Shane stood, using his momentum to add force to a punch he drove into the ghost's ribs, just under the armpit.

"You're going to want to settle down," he advised. He had no interest in fighting the ghost. Tree Man didn't have any information he needed, and he'd just as soon fulfill the ghost's request to leave, but not if the spirit wouldn't stop with the blows.

There was anger in the ghost's eyes as it came at Shane again. Frustrated, Shane swung a right cross, connecting with the ghost's jaw and breaking some growths from his skin. Where they peeled away, the flesh looked like a freshly gouged wound.

"Herbert, you want to talk some sense into your friend?" Shane suggested.

The big ghost was slow to get back to his feet. The branch-like hand had cut small holes into the side of Herbert's face, wounds he'd carry for the rest of his time on Earth.

"I don't really know him. I saw his act once ages ago."

Shane sighed and punched the attacking spirit in the gut again, causing him to double over. An uppercut to the face knocked him straight back to the road, stunned by the attack and vulnerable.

Seizing the momentary advantage, Shane pressed his foot down on the ghost's throat.

"Hold still," he suggested, stopping Tree Man before he raised his fists again.

The other ghosts in the cemetery had come close to the wall to watch the fight unfold. He could see the surprise on their faces with the realization that Shane was both alive and able to harm them. Shane was happier knowing they had a reason to fear him.

"Please, don't hurt him anymore," a ghost in the crowd asked. She was a very old woman, small and wizened and very skeletal with only faint wisps of hair on her head.

"Happy to, if he's willing to relax for a moment."

"He will. Won't you, Basil?" the old lady said.

Tree Man growled and raised his arms again. Shane pressed harder on his throat, causing him to stop.

"Basil," the woman said firmly before looking at Shane. "He's afraid is all. Fear makes him angry. It haunts him as much as he haunts this place. The fear, and the torment, and the pain. His life was hard. His death is no less so."

"Like I said, we're just passing through," Shane replied.

"Then please. Have mercy. He had none in life. Grant him some in death."

Shane looked down at the ghost, holding eye contact for a heartbeat.

"You need to work on keeping calm," he said, letting his foot up. He backed away a step and let the Tree Man get back to his feet.

"Go home, Basil," the old woman ordered. There was still a hint of softness in her voice, but her tone was unmistakably one closed to discussion. Tree Man grunted but did as he was told, averting his eyes as he stalked back to the cemetery like a scolded child.

The other ghosts drifted back to the shadows as the Tree Man retreated, leaving Shane with Herbert and the old woman. Shane retrieved a new cigarette and lit it while the elderly ghost touched the wounds on Herbert's cheek as though she might somehow make them feel better.

"Basil is not an evil man. He's just been through so much. Most of them here have. The world was rarely kind to the children of Roland Hills. Was it kind to you?"

She spoke to Herbert, who smiled and pulled her hand from his face.

"Kind enough, ma'am," he replied.

"No need to lie; I know the pain. The doubt and anger and hate. I saw it build in Basil the same as in so many others. A person can only be an object of ridicule and abuse for so long before it changes who you are down to your soul. Poisons the well, in a way. Takes a long time to fix that damage if it can be fixed at all."

"Life as a carny, you mean?" Shane asked.

"Life as a thing. As less than human."

"I made it through alright," Herbert pointed out. "I had a good run."

"Of course you did, dear," she said. "Made money, right? Entertained people and traveled everywhere. Everyone has the same excuses, don't they? Like the sweet frosting on a cake that's too bitter to swallow."

"I don't think anyone is meant to have a life of just that frosting, ma'am," Herbert countered. "And for people like us—like me—there were never many good choices."

"See how they make you look at who you are? Why were there so few choices? Why have you accepted that you were destined to be taunted, put on display, and made to be insulted and abused?"

Herbert chuckled dryly and spread his arms slightly as though to give a better look at himself.

"I was never going to be a sprinter, ma'am. Or a businessman."

"And Basil, he would never be a writer with his hands, hmm? That doesn't mean you had to be called a freak. What right does anyone have? What about any of that made you less human?"

Shane could see that her words cut Herbert. The big man had been comfortable telling his story, and with the idea of being a freak, but there was more behind it. More that Herbert the man had felt, no matter what spin he put on it.

He and the others in the sideshow, the ones who didn't alter themselves to fit a role the way Diablo had, were trying to take control of something beyond theirs. Shane could understand that. He could also understand how that would have taken a toll. New faces entering a tent to look at you, make fun of you, or laugh at you because you were different.

Shane had come across many ghosts that were different in death than they had been in life. The process of leaving a mortal life behind could have profound changes. In some spirits, it triggered something very powerful, and very dark. A violent death could do it, or a substantial loss. A thirst for vengeance, like in Lisette's case.

A lifetime of being a thing to be mocked had to have affected how one returned as a spirit, too. Even if Herbert seemed like an average or even decent man, Shane didn't doubt there was some darkness there. Maybe not deep or homicidal. But something.

The two ghosts spoke to each other while Shane smoked. He didn't often put a lot of thought into what happened before, why a ghost was the way it was. It often didn't matter, especially if he was in a fight for his life. If a ghost wanted to kill him, and seemed intent on it like Tree Man had, Shane would fight back, destroying the ghost if he had to. He wasn't a therapist for the dead. His job was not to help get to the root of their anger.

But for the second time since coming to Roland Hills, a spirit made

Shane ponder the town of Burkitt. What had pushed those ghosts to that point? With so many spirits, all seemingly very dangerous and angry, it was probably just a snowball effect. One deadly spirit killed others, and they killed others, and the whole town got swallowed up in death and darkness.

But what started that ball rolling?

Towns did not get haunted like that. Even houses didn't get haunted like Burkitt. The core of Burkitt was something wrong but unique. What made a spirit that dark?

"Watch yourselves," the old woman said as Herbert left her. "There are angrier folks than Basil out and about in Roland Hills."

Shane offered her a nod and turned to follow Herbert, who had taken the lead on the way back to Rags' home.

"You okay?" Shane asked. The big ghost was looking a little more stone-faced than usual, and it was rare for him to be so intent on getting anywhere ahead of Shane.

"We should have stayed in the house," Herbert said, his eyes downcast.

"Could have been worse. The face scars give you character," Shane replied.

Herbert raised a hand, touched his face, and shook his head.

"Not that. It's this place. Those people. I don't want to be around people like that."

"Ghosts?" Shane asked.

"Victims," Herbert replied. "Self-pitying victims."

The big ghost's tone was as harsh as Shane had ever heard, and it surprised him.

"I take it you don't sympathize with the plight of the Tree Man," Shane said, exhaling a puff of smoke as he looked back. The ghosts were gone.

"I've heard it before. 'You poor man, what a horrible life. People can be cruel; you deserve better.' It's nonsense. Coping mechanisms for the weak."

Shane grunted. Herbert was fully angry now.

"Is it bad that people made fun of Tree Man? Exploited him for money, treated him like a monster? Of course. It's bad that people get hit by cars, too. Or beaten by their parents or abandoned by their spouses. A million bad things happen to a million people every day. You don't mope all the way to the afterlife about it. You don't act like there was a secret utopia of kindness and joy waiting on the other side of a fence you could never reach. The world sucked for a lot of people."

"So your philosophy, if I may summarize, is, 'Life sucks, deal with it.'"

Herbert looked at Shane with a scowl on his face, and it was the first truly angry expression Shane had seen on the ghost since they met. It wasn't tainted by fear or confusion. Just anger. Shane had to laugh, and after a moment of trying to hold his resolve, the ghost laughed with him.

"My word, is that what I sound like?" he asked.

"A little bit," Shane confirmed. Herbert shook his head and sighed.

"It's not that. I just don't want to blame others for my problems. Whatever I had thrown at me by others, or life itself, doesn't change me. No one controls me. No one controlled me. I think it's a crutch, and I don't need it."

"Herbert the Crutchless Ghost," Shane said with an approving nod. "Doesn't need anyone's damn pity."

"No, I don't," he agreed.

"I like you, Herbert. You remind me of a friend back home."

Herbert smiled, and they turned down the road toward Rags' home. It was dark now, and a scattered few ghosts watched them from windows and shadows. A scattered few living did as well, but they paid them little mind.

"Wasn't sure you had real friends," Herbert said.

"Getting a little salty now, Herbert," Shane said. The big man laughed again, and they continued to Rags' house.

Giselle was still supervising Rags on a thorough cleanup of the place, but they had finished in the spare bedroom. Shane left them to it and after quickly grabbing something to eat, he hit the bedroom and shut out the noise of Rags and Giselle thumping around the rest of the house.

With any luck, Roland Hills would be in the rearview mirror soon enough.

CHAPTER 7
PURSUIT

"Lake Placid."

Shane awoke with a start and opened his eyes to see Herbert looming over him in the bed.

"What?" he said.

"The carnival was in Lake Placid. We were practically right there."

Shane put a hand out to force the ghost back and sat up. They had been less than an hour from Lake Placid when they left New York. Of course, they'd had no way to know that, so the carnival might as well have been on the dark side of the moon.

"They're still there?" Shane asked.

"Mr. Rags' friend says they started packing up this morning."

Shane got out of bed and followed Herbert downstairs. Giselle was gone, and the house was considerably tidier than it had been the day before. Still a total mess to most normal people, but relatively speaking, it was a stark improvement.

"If you hurry, you won't be too far behind," Rags said as Shane entered the living room. He threw something that Shane caught instinctively, then turned over to look at it. A set of keys.

"Thank you," Shane said. The old man shrugged.

"Not like I got anywhere to drive to. You better refill the tank before you return it, though. She's parked around back."

"We will. Thank you, Rags. I mean that," Herbert said. Rags nodded and took a sip from a very-early-morning beer.

"Make sure your friend doesn't die. Good luck."

Shane went out the back door and into the dim light of early morning. A handful of vehicles were in the back just as there had been in the front, but the nearest was a beat-down old blue pickup truck with rusted panels. It was the only one that looked even remotely driveable.

Shane hopped in the driver's seat and turned the key. The engine roared to life with some sputters and rattling sounds, making Shane a little nervous about its overall fitness. Rags was not great at house maintenance, and his vehicle care might have suffered, too.

Herbert took up the passenger seat and Shane put the car in gear, driving off the property and back out of town the way they'd come. They'd have to backtrack almost the entire trip from New York and a little extra, but he hoped that would only put them an hour or two behind the carnival.

The truck had some power under the hood despite its lackluster appearance and Shane pressed it as much as he could when he felt safe to do so. The back roads would be relatively free of cops, and he was willing to risk speeding when and where he could. Once he got to the main roads, he wouldn't risk it. The last thing he wanted was to blunder into police custody over a traffic violation.

They reached Lake Placid in less than three hours, shaving off considerable time by using side roads to avoid people on their morning commutes. By the time they rolled into the tourist village, it was just starting its day.

Herbert directed Shane to a spot on the outskirts of McKenzie Mountain Wilderness, where Rags' contact had seen the carnival set up. It was a vast area of park used for camping and hiking off the western shore of Lake Placid, and when they arrived, it was stomped flat and vacant.

There were signs the carnival had been there, including garbage cans full of old popcorn and drink cups and ruts in the grass and dirt from countless vehicles. With no way to know how much of a head start the carnival had or which direction it had gone, Shane was frustrated that they were back in the same hole they'd been in before going to Roland Hills.

"Right there," Herbert said suddenly, pointing at something ahead of them.

Shane had pulled into the lot where the carnival had been set up, and there was nothing to see at first glance. They were removed from any populated areas, and there were no homes or businesses nearby. But someone was standing at the forest's edge watching them.

"That looks unpleasant," Herbert said.

The ghost at the edge of the forest looked like he had been partially eaten. His clothes hung in torn, bloodied scraps, and his flesh, from his face to his exposed torso to his thighs, was marred by bites, bloody scratches, and wounds. If Shane had to guess, he'd say the man had been mauled to death by a bear.

"Seen worse," Shane said, getting out of the truck. Herbert grimaced and followed.

The ghost did not come to them, but he didn't shy away, either. He stayed just inside the tree line, across the vacant lot, and watched them approach.

On closer inspection, the ghost's condition was grislier than it had first appeared. He must have been in his twenties when he died, but his injuries were horrendous. His left eye and most of the flesh and bone around it had been torn away, exposing the interior of his skull and brain. Scrapes and cuts and bites covered more than half of his exposed flesh. Whatever had happened had not been quick or painless.

"Hello," Shane said, offering a quick wave after lighting a cigarette.

"You're from the carnival," the ghost said, his voice crackling like someone suffering a bad chest infection.

"How did you know that?" Herbert asked. The ghost's one eye took in Herbert from head to toe.

"Not many ghosts spending time with the living around here. Now I see it two days in a row."

"You saw them? Was the ghost cloaked in shadow?" Herbert asked.

The mauled ghost looked them over again.

"Yes. You're… not with them?" he asked.

"*Looking* for them," Shane clarified. "How long ago did they leave?"

Though the ghost's face was so ruined it was hard to gauge his expressions, Shane had the distinct impression this one was suspicious.

"Why do you want to know?" he asked.

"We're friends. Looking to catch up," Herbert replied. The ghost's ruined face became stony, and Shane removed the cigarette from between his lips.

"That's not entirely true," he said, netting him a frown from Herbert. "They killed a bunch of people, and I'm hoping to catch up and destroy the ghost before she can do it again."

"Shane, what are—"

"Yeah," the ruined ghost said before Herbert could continue. "That makes sense."

"What makes sense?" Herbert asked.

"Your 'friends'. I saw the ghost get into a fight with the man in the top hat. It didn't speak, not that I heard. He was yelling and trying to convince it to leave some people alone. Said it needed to get control of itself and that they couldn't keep doing what they were doing."

"He talked her out of something?" Herbert asked. The other ghost shook his head.

"No. He tried to talk it out of killing people. But it happened anyway."

"Who?" Shane asked.

"Looked like customers. Just people having fun at the carnival. Must have done something to set that ghost off, though."

"What happened?" Herbert asked softly.

"The night went on. Got late; they started shutting down. These two people, a man and a woman, were heading on their way out and once they left the grounds, the ghost sneaked out after them and killed them. Top hat man had to drag them back and stash their bodies in a truck."

"But why? Why would she keep killing people?" Herbert asked, more of Shane than the ghost who had witnessed it.

"It's what she is now, Herbert. Anything, any slight, is going to set her off. She doesn't need reasons anymore."

"Must not be the first time, I can tell you that," the ghost added. "That truck had other bodies in it."

Herbert turned away, shaking his head.

"How long since they left?" he asked.

"Not long. Two hours, maybe less? They headed west toward eighty-six. Didn't seem to be in a big rush the way you'd expect people with a truckload of dead bodies to be. I mean, the top hat guy waited until morning to even get going."

West was what Shane and Herbert had predicted, but they had a road now, and a solid route to follow. And with only a two-hour delay, there was a good chance they could still catch up.

"Thanks for the help," Shane told the ghost before doubling back to the truck. Herbert was quickly at his side but still distraught over the news that Lisette had not stopped her killing spree. The truck engine struggled to life again with a painful whine and rattle before settling into a smooth rumble.

The carnival would not and could not push the speed limit with the Ferris wheel and a truck full of corpses. They wouldn't risk any exposure, which gave Shane and Herbert a bit of a leg up.

They headed west when they reached route eighty-six. There was no way to know the carnival's destination, but if Lisette had killed again, Hartwell would want distance between themselves and where it happened. They'd devote time to traveling farther rather than finding a spot nearby, which would give Shane more time to hunt them down without worrying about turning onto random side roads and into small towns.

The heavily wooded countryside was serene and calm, providing a contrast to the horror they were pursuing. Every minute that ticked by and mile that clicked on the odometer increased the tension. Neither Shane nor Herbert had much to say. They rode in silence, keeping their eyes on the road and the surrounding countryside.

It was only when route eighty-six came to a major crossroads at Saranac Lake that they pulled over at a service station. The attendant inside remembered the carnival as the convoy had stopped there to gas up before continuing down eighty-six through town less than an hour before.

Shane drove cautiously through the town and then up past Lake Colby. They were headed north again, and he wasn't sure how long he wanted to follow the road. Hartwell probably wanted to leave the state, so he'd need to get back on a westerly track as soon as he could.

"What's that?" Herbert asked as they passed the lake and returned to the forested countryside. Smoke rose above the trees in puffy, black wisps in the near distance. They were far from the town and even from any houses beyond the lake, in the center of the forest with little else around. Some might have dismissed it as a campfire, but the smoke looked too thick and too dark. Something large was burning.

"Not sure," Shane said, detouring down the nearest road toward the smoke. They lost sight of it for several minutes among the looming trees until they came to a farmer's field in a clear-cut portion of the forest. Whatever had been growing in the clearing was still small, barely more than sprouts. The crop was all but destroyed now, however, thanks to the smoldering remains of trucks and vans scattered across the field.

The Ferris wheel truck was burning the brightest, but flames had gutted the other vehicles. Tents and supplies had been scattered and burned as well, thrown haphazardly to the ground, and set alight. The carnival had not been set up, from what Shane could see. Not even an attempt had been made. They had simply piled into the field and burned it all.

"Why would they agree to this?" Herbert asked, dumbfounded. Shane pulled Rags' truck up to the side of the field, as close to the flaming wreckage as he could without risking their ride, and scanned the burning remnants.

"They didn't," he said.

Bodies were strewn among the burning trucks and supplies. Charred black and smoking, with a few still burning, Shane saw at least a half-dozen from where he sat in the truck.

The ghost at Lake Placid had claimed there was a truck of bodies, but Shane wasn't convinced these were the same ones. These were workers, the roustabouts, and others who had been a part of the carnival. Something must have happened to set Lisette off, or maybe Hartwell had finally hit his breaking point. Whatever the case, Bartolomy and Sons was no more.

Herbert left the truck to investigate the carnage. Shane followed, forced to keep more of a distance to avoid the heat and smoke. As he moved around the outer edges, more bodies came into view. They had eradicated everyone.

"Shane," Herbert called.

He stood near a truck that Shane could barely see through the smoke. It was one of the twenty-six-foot-long moving trucks that hauled some of the carnival's larger pieces of equipment. Through the haze, Shane could see that its purpose had been changed at some point. The door had been rolled up, and the back was stuffed with bodies.

"It's Shiva. And Bernard and Lobo and everyone. My friends," Herbert said, his voice cracking as he covered his mouth. "They killed them all."

The wind shifted and blew smoke into Shane's face. He winced from the sting but also the smell. The acrid scent of burning chemicals mixed with the smell of burned meat. He stepped back, scowling, and nearly tripped over something in the ditch behind him.

"God. You," a strained voice said.

Shane looked down at Diablo. Most of his tattoos were gone, burned away by fire, and across his face, by a black handprint. One horn had been pulled from his skull, exposing bone, and he bled from a dozen wounds.

"Herbert," Shane called, crouching next to the man. He had open wounds over nearly his entire body. They could offer no aid. He doubted the man would survive even in a hospital given his state. That he was alive at all was hard to believe.

"What happened here? Why did they do this?" he asked. Diablo grinned and the black flesh on his face cracked and oozed.

"Can't say. Police released me just after you. Made my way back and heard about Artemis. Thought maybe I could... I don't know. Didn't matter. Didn't work."

Herbert arrived and gasped, collapsing next to his friend.

"Oh, good Lord, Diablo," he said before looking up at Shane. "We have to call an ambulance."

"Big man," Diablo said as though scolding. "Too late for that."

"You're going to die," Herbert said softly.

"Yeah," Diablo agreed. He looked past Herbert at Shane. "You gotta stop her."

"Where did they go?" Shane asked.

"I don't know. She's not... she's a monster now. She's trying to save kids, she says. She's protecting kids. Killing anyone... anyone who she thinks hurts kids."

"You never hurt kids," Herbert said. "No one here hurt people."

"Doesn't matter. Not to her. All in her head now."

He exhaled loudly, and the breath kept coming, slow and steady, much longer than it should have. Herbert kept talking to him, telling him it would be okay and that they could find help.

He didn't know Diablo was already dead.

CHAPTER 8

THE NOOSE

The sound of sirens in the distance came on the breeze a few moments later. Someone else had seen the smoke, and emergency crews would be there soon. Police would swarm the area once they saw the bodies. Once they knew it was the carnival and how it connected to Shane and the other murders, the FBI wouldn't be far behind. They had to leave quickly.

"Herbert, we can't stay," Shane warned, getting back into the truck.

The ghost touched the face of his friend. It had been a long while since Shane had seen anyone look so lost and heartbroken as the big ghost. Many spirits had tempered emotions; some seemed to have left them behind entirely. Herbert wore his heart on his sleeve, and it was in tatters.

To his credit, the ghost understood the risk and left Diablo and the others without complaint. Shane turned the key once Herbert was in the truck. The engine struggled and rumbled. It sputtered several times and then went dead.

"What's wrong?" Herbert asked.

Shane clenched his jaw and turned the key again, giving the truck more gas. Belts whined, and the engine sputtered. Something snapped loudly, and the engine went dead. On the third try, turning the key only produced a clicking sound.

"You've got to be kidding," Shane growled.

"What happened?" Herbert demanded, half in a panic. Shane left the truck and circled it. The ghost followed him as he crossed the road.

"We have to run," he said. There was no chance of making it anywhere on the road; they'd be caught in minutes. The forest opposite the field at least had the potential to lead them somewhere. If nothing else, it offered cover.

Shane did not know how far they were from civilization. The nearest town could have been a ten-minute walk or six hours, and guessing the best direction to avoid police was a crapshoot.

Lights flashed at the end of the street and Shane ducked into the woods, crouching low beyond the tree line. Escape would have to wait until he had more freedom to move. He didn't want to draw undue attention unless he had to.

Obscured behind ferns alongside a cluster of maple and birch trees, he watched as a firetruck and an ambulance pulled up to the flaming remains of the carnival.

Men and women in uniform scattered and set about their duties. A hose was attached to the tanker while a paramedic yelled for help, having discovered Diablo's body.

Police and a second fire engine arrived within minutes. Water roared as they hosed down the trucks and vans and Shane stayed hidden, not moving a muscle.

At least five state police cars were on the scene before an unmarked vehicle pulled up. The bodies had all been discovered, but fire crews still needed to put out the fires and lower the temperature before any of them could be retrieved.

A man got out of the unmarked car. His suit was plain, and he wore eighties-style sunglasses. His hair was slightly disheveled, and he was young; Shane guessed mid-twenties. But the car and the suit were a dead giveaway. He was FBI.

The agent stood in the center of the road as emergency crews worked around him. He did nothing for a long moment, just stood with his hands on his hips. Then, as though noticing it for the first time, he approached Rags' pickup.

"Rags is going to be so angry," Herbert said. He was crouched and hiding with Shane, though it was unnecessary for him to do so.

"Hey!" one of the police officers yelled, finally noticing the man inspecting the truck. The agent didn't acknowledge the officer and instead searched the glove box.

"Let me see your hands!" the officer yelled, drawing his sidearm. Other officers took note and followed their coworkers' lead, drawing guns.

The agent turned his head, looking out at everyone from behind his sunglasses.

"What's your name?" he asked.

"Hands. Now," the officer replied.

"My hands are attached to my wrists. Is there a brain attached to your mouth?" the agent said, getting back to inspecting the truck.

"On your knees, smart guy," the cop instructed. The agent took a step away from the truck.

"Xander Ventura," he said loudly. "I'm a federal agent pursuing a suspect tied to this case, and you are wasting valuable time I could put to better use tracking down what might be one of the most prolific serial killers in American history. Who's your supervisor?"

The officer looked at another officer, who shrugged. Neither lowered their weapons.

"Come and check my ID and badge already," Ventura ordered.

One officer came forward cautiously after getting a nod from the loudmouth cop. He patted Ventura down, pulling a gun from a side holster, and then his wallet from his jacket pocket.

"Says he's FBI," the officer said, turning the ID toward the other cop.

"Yes, it does," Ventura said, holding out his hand. The officer handed back the wallet and gun. The other officers lowered their weapons and approached him. No longer fearful that the man was a suspect, they lowered their voices and Shane couldn't hear what they were saying.

"That must be the man who contacted your friend," Herbert said.

"Likely," Shane whispered. He was working alone, which struck him as odd.

After a chat with the police, they returned to securing the scene and left Ventura alone for a moment. Shane watched as the agent's body slumped and he leaned forward, hands on his knees, and took a deep breath.

"That man was terrified," he continued. He'd put on a brave enough show in front of the other cops, but it looked like it was all a show. He looked like he needed a bathroom and a stiff drink, in that order. "Can you get a little closer, listen in on what he's doing?"

Herbert looked surprised.

"Me?"

"Of course you. No one can see you," Shane reminded him.

The ghost nodded and got to his feet.

"I'll be back soon. Just… wait here."

Herbert strolled out of the woods, trying to look casual as though it mattered. Shane shook his head and watched as the big man made his way from the woods to the assembled emergency workers and their vehicles, weaving closer to the scene like he was meant to be there.

Herbert had not spent much time exploiting any of the features of being a ghost. He was used to most of his friends in the carnival being fully aware of where he was and interacting with him. Sneaking around and being invisible to most eyes was not something he had considered, and therefore, it did not come naturally.

Those days were over now, he realized. He would never go back to the carnival. He'd never see his friends again. There was no one left. The only people he could consider friends anymore were, well, no one but Shane Ryan.

Shane might not have been his first choice of companion, but he had been nothing if not honest. He was trying to help, even if they kept hitting brick walls. But worse was that he had become another victim of Lisette, of the carnival, for getting involved. The police and the FBI thought he was responsible. Herbert hated he had done that to the man. He would find a way to clear his name. He had to.

The FBI agent was directing some officers around the scene of the fire, pointing out bodies in the wreckage or things he wanted them to take into evidence. He was on the phone between, seemingly speaking to everyone at once.

"Ryan," Ventura said. "They'd picked him up in Nashua and Detroit. He's been neck-deep in murders and disappearances for years. He'll turn up somewhere; he always does."

Ventura nodded as he listened to whoever was on the other end of the line. Herbert casually moved closer, eyes fixed on the accident scene like he was another onlooker.

"Sir, if you could—" He stopped abruptly and nodded. "Yes, but…"
Another pause followed.

"Yes, sir. Understood," the agent said before hanging up with a frustrated sigh. He slipped the phone back into his pocket.

Herbert took another sideways step closer, bridging the gap between them to just a couple of yards. Ventura turned and looked in Herbert's direction. His brow furrowed, and he lifted the sunglasses from his eyes.

"Who are you?" he asked. Herbert kept his eyes fixed on the carnival.

"Sir?" one of the nearby officers asked. Ventura shook his head.

"You. Who are you?"

The officer frowned and turned around, looking to see if someone was behind him. Herbert turned his head slightly and made eye contact. Ventura waved at him.

"Yeah, who the hell are you? Don't tell me you're a cop from this neck of the woods."

"Are you alright, sir?" the cop asked.

Herbert stared into Ventura's eyes and froze. The agent was looking right at him, there was no mistake. He could see Herbert as clearly as Herbert could see him.

Tentatively, Herbert took a step backward.

"What is going… on…?" Ventura said. His confusion seemed to fade and his eyes widened. Herbert saw the realization dawn on him. Ventura could see the dead and realized who Herbert was. Or *what* he was.

The police officer was about to speak again when Ventura waved him off.

"Sorry, officer, uh… Bluetooth," Ventura said, pointing at his ear. "Wasn't talking to you."

The cop seemed to accept that as an answer and returned to what he'd been doing. Herbert, for his part, turned his back on Ventura. If the agent could see him, he couldn't return to Shane. He also couldn't lead the man away. Shane held the cameo necklace that bound Herbert to the world in his pocket. He could travel a mile away at best. It would have to do.

He began walking casually from the crowd of emergency workers, following the road away from the scene. He kept his eyes forward, not even wanting to look at Shane to give away his location. He had to throw off the FBI agent.

Ventura followed behind him. Like Herbert, he was trying to be casual. As much as Herbert didn't want to be seen, it looked like Ventura didn't want anyone to know he had seen a ghost, which made sense. FBI agents talking about ghosts probably lost their jobs fairly quickly.

Herbert kept a steady pace. He enjoyed walking when he could. It was not the sort of luxury he enjoyed much when he was alive because of his size and the discomfort it caused. He could wander freely now as a ghost and often liked to check out the new places where the carnival stopped, back before Lisette had been released. It was rather peaceful to do it again.

Ventura paced him, not wanting to draw eyes as he caught up. Herbert could only hope Shane was watching and understood what was happening.

The farther he walked the faster Ventura moved, trying to close the gap and losing any fear that the police could see what he was up to.

"Hey," the agent called out once they were far enough from the others to not be heard. "Hey. Please stop for a minute."

Herbert didn't look back and instead picked up the pace. If he could get away, he could duck into the woods and double back to Shane. No one had to see anything. He just needed to lose Ventura.

"Hey!" the FBI agent shouted again. He broke into a run. Herbert could hear his footfalls and dared a look back. Ventura was already on him, holding his hands out in a non-threatening way as he caught up and then circled the ghost, stopping in front of him.

"I just... wow," he said, catching his breath.

Herbert looked around nervously. He was not a fan of violence, but he probably could have knocked the man out. He didn't want to kill him; that seemed like too much. And they might blame Shane for it. But maybe a firm strike on the head would knock him unconscious.

"You're a ghost," Ventura said. It was not clear if it was a question.

The agent seemed half terrified and half in awe. Herbert wondered how many ghosts he'd seen, as his reaction made it seem like this was a novel occurrence.

"Are you from the carnival? Were you a... worker? A victim of what happened?"

Herbert said nothing. If the man thought he was mute, he might leave him alone. That was better than beating him unconscious.

"Please. Do you know who did this? Where I can find him? It is Shane Ryan, isn't it? I can help you get justice."

He was determined if nothing else. Herbert started walking again, heading right for him. Maybe a quick scare was all he needed.

Ventura jumped back quickly, pulling something from his pocket. It appeared to be a simple metal rod, a chunk of iron, maybe.

"Don't make me use this," Ventura said, holding up the iron and preparing to strike. He spoke the threat in a manner that made Herbert think the man knew what iron did to a ghost.

They stared each other down. Ventura was nervous, his breathing rapid, and his eye movement unfocused. Herbert wondered if he'd ever confronted a ghost so directly. His face was flushed, and he kept adjusting his grip on the iron bar.

Herbert needed to get away from the agent and back to Shane undetected. The solution was obvious. He ran at Ventura.

The FBI agent's eyes widened and panic set in. He took a step back and held out the iron bar like some kind of shield. Herbert's charge was swift and surprising. His bulk made him appear slow and ponderous, but being a ghost meant he was not restrained by any real physical limitations.

Ventura steeled himself, firming his grip on the iron. Herbert reached for it, swiping his hand through the air as though trying to swat a fly. He hit the iron bar with the flat of his palm and was gone.

CHAPTER 9
RUN FOR YOUR LIFE

Shane jumped over a downed tree, darted past a tangle of wild raspberries, and skidded down an embankment. His lungs were already burning, and not for the first time, he wondered why he spent so much time smoking.

The sound of his pulse was in his ears, and any time he paused for even a moment, a cloud of gnats and mosquitoes settled on his head to feast on his flesh.

He needed distance between himself and Herbert. His hiding spot probably would have kept him safe for a little while, at least until the coast was clear enough to make a more relaxed getaway, but that agent had seen Herbert. The man could see ghosts and Shane was willing to bet the next pack of cigarettes he shouldn't be smoking that he didn't know Herbert was one, at least at first.

Ventura had spoken to Herbert, and Shane had seen the realization dawn on the man's face. He could see Herbert but did not realize what he was at first. Shane could always pick a ghost out of a crowd, but this man could not. At least not one that looked like a normal person the way Herbert did.

In terms of the murders, there was no way to know what the implications of an FBI agent who could see ghosts would be, but Shane wasn't eager to find out. At worst, he'd still be arrested as the prime suspect. But there was now a clear possibility that Ventura would get himself killed, too.

Herbert's haunted cameo was still in Shane's pocket. He knew the ghost couldn't get back to him without drawing attention from Ventura and leading him to Shane, but Shane could force the issue with distance. Herbert would have to come to him if he was separated from the cameo by too great a distance.

Shane was not keen on running a mile through the woods, but it was the only solution he could think of. It also put distance between himself and law enforcement, which he needed.

His feet slid through a pile of damp leaves, and he nearly lost his balance. Gasping from the effort, he paused at a birch tree to catch his breath. The papery bark flaked under the pressure of his hand when Herbert suddenly appeared before him.

"Where are we?" he said, turning around to take in the forest.

Shane raised an eyebrow and looked over his shoulder. He had not yet run a mile.

"How did you get here?"

"That agent," Herbert said, pointing in the wrong direction. "He had an iron bar. I don't think he knows exactly what it does to a ghost."

"He attacked you?" Shane asked.

"I attacked him," the big ghost corrected. Shane chuckled and nodded.

"Good plan."

"He knew I was a ghost. Not at first, but he realized it. What if he discovers Lisette before we do?"

"What do you think?" Shane replied.

"He's going to die."

Herbert was not wrong. It made Shane wonder if Ventura had requested this case because he knew something or thought he did. Seemed like too much of a coincidence that the man had been assigned the case and that he could see ghosts. But if his ability to do so was so clumsy and unreliable that he could talk to a ghost and not realize it, then Herbert was right. He would stand no chance against a spirit like Lisette.

The last thing Shane wanted to do was babysit an FBI agent who had developed a hankering to investigate paranormal cases. He didn't want the potential murder of that agent blamed on him, either. Everything was becoming far more complicated than it needed to be.

"Come on. We have to find Hartwell and Lisette," Shane said, continuing through the woods at a more reasonable pace.

"Do you know where we're going?" Herbert asked.

"Have to hit a road eventually, right?" Shane said.

The ghost was unconvinced.

"This forest could cover hundreds of square miles."

"We were headed in this direction when we turned off the main road to investigate the smoke. The road had to be headed somewhere. We'll find something."

"As long as you're sure," Herbert said, doubt in his voice.

Shane was not sure, but he was confident enough. They were in New York. They'd find a town or a road or something if they stayed on course.

There was no way to know why Hartwell and the ghost had destroyed the carnival and killed the workers, but he bet they went to ground afterward. Hartwell would want to be out of sight; maybe Lisette would, too. Something serious must have happened for them to take such drastic action.

"What's going to happen if we find them?" Herbert asked after a long pause.

The sounds of the woods had long since replaced any distant sirens, and though birds and animals would avoid Herbert's presence, there were enough elsewhere in the woods to make the forest seem very much alive. It was oddly relaxing, given how stressful fleeing police through a forest was.

"You already know what's going to happen," Shane assured him. It was a strange question for the ghost to ask after the time they'd spent together.

"You were only really focused on Lisette before, but Bart had to have done this. The fire. Some of those deaths. They weren't all frozen black."

Herbert kept his eyes forward and Shane nodded.

Until now, Hartwell had been more passive in his assistance. That was no longer the case.

"What are you asking me, Herbert?" Shane said.

He knew, but he wanted Herbert to commit to what he was asking.

"Are you going to kill Bart Hartwell?"

That was the crux of things. Lisette was a foregone conclusion. She had to be destroyed, and it was unlikely anyone else would come along who could handle that job. In theory, any ghost could do it. Herbert could destroy her, but Shane didn't think he had it in him. And really, that was just a technical thing. Ghosts could destroy each other. Lisette was probably too powerful for Herbert. Shane had seen her in action. She was strong and ruthless. Herbert was not.

Hartwell was just a man. He could be held responsible for the crimes he had committed, and the people he had killed. But how could the justice system of the living reconcile what had happened with his level of involvement? It wouldn't make sense. He'd never be able to account for how everyone died, or why. And they'd never believe the truth.

There was a chance Hartwell would get railroaded, and they'd overlook the parts of the crimes they couldn't explain, hold him accountable, and imprison him. There was just as much chance any legal case would get thrown out, or he'd be found not competent to stand trial if he insisted on telling stories about ghosts.

The simplest justice would come from Shane. He could kill Hartwell. It was no less than the man deserved. Hartwell had murdered dozens of people, directly or indirectly. He was as much a monster as Lisette. And if his excuse was that he loved her, Shane wasn't buying it. He didn't care.

"If I have to," Shane answered.

He would not commit to any plan yet. How could he? They didn't know where Hartwell or Lisette were, or what they were doing. For all they knew, Hartwell was one of those burned corpses. Shane didn't believe it, but anything was possible.

"Good," Herbert replied.

Shane could hear the lack of conviction in the ghost's voice. Not that Shane doubted Herbert wanted him dead. He had just lost his entire world, everyone he had ever called friend or family. It must have been hard. The only two people he had left who had been a part of that family were the ones who had destroyed it.

The emotional state of a ghost could be a very fragile thing. Shane had seen how a ghost like Eloise could become violent and change her demeanor on a dime if something set her off. He wondered if Herbert was building up to the same loss of control that turned Lisette into what she had become.

They continued southwest for nearly an hour, heading through the woods toward where Shane believed they would reconnect with the original road they'd been on. Herbert spoke very little on the journey, which suited Shane well enough. He didn't like feeling like he was behind the eight ball and needed time to sort through that. The solution was not apparent, and it frustrated him. He wanted time alone to deal with it, but a silent walk was what he had.

"Do you hear that?" Herbert asked after saying nothing for well over a mile of hiking. Shane stopped to listen. It came from somewhere to their right. The unmistakable sound of tires on pavement and humming engines. There was a road.

He altered course, taking a more direct path to the road until it became clear through the trees as cars passed at irregular intervals, coming and going across his field of vision.

Shane held back from the tree line, not wanting to be seen in case the police were heading to or from the carnival massacre. They had been walking for miles, but it was nothing for a car to have covered the distance in a straight shot.

They stayed hidden, close enough to see and follow the road but far enough that no one was likely to see them. Soon enough, they reached a sign.

"Tillman's in five miles. Ever heard of it?" Shane asked.

Herbert shook his head.

"Looks like it's the only option. We could maybe find a new car there," he suggested.

Shane agreed, and they continued through the trees. Trudging five miles over uneven ground in the forest took longer than he would have liked. Nearly two hours passed before the trees cut away to make room for a shopping center that had been set up on the outskirts of town.

The Tillman Center featured about thirty stores and a parking lot full of cars like a nearly endless vehicle graveyard. It was incredibly public, and ironically, a perfect place to get lost. No one would take notice of Shane among so many other people.

"There," he said, pointing out the automotive center attached to a big box store.

"What?" Herbert asked.

"Need you to move some security cameras there and create a distraction so I can grab a set of keys and get a car."

"Oh," Herbert said. "I can do that."

Shane kept his distance and waited for the ghost to approach the shop. He moved up the walls like a spider, albeit a four-hundred-pound one, and pushed the cameras aside before sneaking into the shop where employees were changing the oil on a car up on a lift. Shane kept his eye on a car parked outside the bay doors, something they'd already finished work on that still had an invoice on the dash.

Herbert made a beeline for the rear of the shop space, and after pausing a moment, he pushed over an entire rack of batteries with a loud crash.

The employees panicked and Shane slipped in, taking a set of keys from a board in the small office before anyone noticed. Herbert was already in the car when Shane unlocked the door and got in.

"That was exciting," the ghost said. Shane grinned and started the engine.

"Glad you enjoyed it," he said.

They left the parking lot, calm and casual, and got onto the road. Shane had no destination in mind and wasn't sure where to begin.

Where would Hartwell take Lisette?

They had driven only a block and stopped at an intersection when Herbert's arm crossed his field of vision.

"Look," he said.

Shane did as instructed. A sign on the street that branched left directed drivers to Tillman Children's Hospital.

"Huh," Shane said.

"You think they saw it?" Herbert asked.

"Think it's the best bet we have for now," Shane said.

If Lisette was obsessing over children and punishing people she thought were harming them, then a children's hospital had to be a prime destination. She could do the most damage while convincing herself she was doing the most good.

It would also make it that much easier for her to find victims.

CHAPTER 10

WHERE DEATH WAITS

Tillman Children's Hospital was on the opposite side of town from where Shane and Herbert had seen the sign. The parking lot was much less impressive than the one at the shopping center, but the facility was still of a decent size and must have served a large section of the area, not just Tillman but in the surrounding county.

The building was old, possibly from the fifties based on the architecture, and Shane could tell it had seen its share of tragedy over the years. A ghost in the parking lot stood still as a statue and stared at the road that led back to the city. Shane could not tell if it had been male or female. It was awash in blood that puddled at its feet. Clear, green eyes were the only feature not saturated red.

"Oh," Herbert said upon seeing it.

"A lot of ghosts carry their death with them," Shane told him.

Herbert's experiences with other ghosts were surprisingly limited. Most of the ones he'd met were average, like him. Ones Ventura might overlook in a crowd. The hospital trip would likely change his perspective.

Like graveyards, hospitals had a habit of collecting the dead. Hospital ghosts often bore signs of an unpleasant end. A children's hospital would probably be worse. He wondered if Lisette knew that. Or if she cared.

Shane pulled the stolen car into a spot and got out, heading with Herbert toward the entrance. The hospital was extremely large and covered a good deal of ground. He didn't count, but there were at least ten floors and two wings attached to a central building. If Lisette was there, their work was cut out for them. Good thing Herbert could take some shortcuts.

"They're not going to like me wandering around this place alone," Shane said, approaching the door.

"What do you mean? I assume sick children would love a visit from you," Herbert replied. He could not keep a straight face and, despite being the butt of the joke, Shane was pleased to see he had kept a sense of humor. Herbert's potential turn to the dark side would not come just yet.

"Hilarious," Shane said. "But it's less the kids and more the staff. People don't like strange men wandering through hospitals, especially in restricted areas."

"So that's my territory, you mean?" Herbert asked.

"Check the basement, the staff-only sections, any place out of sight where Hartwell could hide. Lisette will probably be close. I'll stick to open areas as much as I can. Find me if you find anything. Either way, let's meet at the cafeteria in an hour, and we'll regroup."

"Got it. What if they find me?" Herbert asked. They'd reached the front doors and Shane looked at the ghost.

"Don't let her rip off your head."

Shane opened the door and headed inside. A handful of people sat reading in chairs; others wandered to and from elevators. Herbert stood for a moment in front of a board that gave directions and then headed down a hall to their right. Shane went left, casual but focused, looking like a man who was supposed to be there and knew where he was going.

He headed down halls and glanced into rooms, never straggling for long or looking lost. Hospital staff were often far too busy to care what a person in motion was doing. If he was walking, it meant he was going somewhere, and that made him all but invisible to staff, including security. Loitering was a danger, so he avoided it.

The first several hallways he saw had nothing to offer. They were too front-and-center, anyway. If Lisette was there, she'd want a base of operations, and that meant keeping Hartwell out of sight if he was still alive.

Shane would have investigated the basement if he could have; that was the most promising option. The hospital was old enough that it likely had a large boiler room or at least a complex underground network of rooms and storage areas that the public was not allowed access to. Places that would have been ideal for a ghost. He hoped Herbert was giving them a thorough run-through. If not, he'd have to gain access later.

Shane navigated through the first floor of the hospital's north wing and found a bank of elevators. He followed the signs and headed to the fourth floor to scout out the cafeteria. There were only so many places where the public could hang out at all hours and not look out of place, and the cafeteria was the best choice for Hartwell.

A quick search turned up nothing suspicious. Shane went on his way, traveling through halls full of exam rooms, diagnostic labs, patient rooms, and more, never lingering longer than he needed to.

Patients watched him pass and he looked casual, just another family member searching for his child or nephew or family friend. No one worth a second glance.

There were surprisingly few ghosts in the hospital during this initial run. He'd often seen one or two stragglers haunting rooms, roaming hallways, or standing in corners doing not much at all.

A ghost would at least be able to offer insight into where he could look for others, if they'd seen Lisette, or where Shane might go to look for someone trying not to be seen. It wasn't the sort of question he could ask the living. But aside from the bloody ghost in the parking lot, he found none.

When an hour had passed and he'd found nothing of interest, Shane returned to the cafeteria and sat with a vending machine coffee. It tasted like bitter water that was somehow burned, and he felt sympathy for families who had to spend a long time there with only that to drink.

People filtered through slowly, speaking in quiet voices the way people do in hospitals. He watched a doctor eat a meal alone, his eyes locked on his phone the whole time, and then a couple with a toddler trying to get the child to eat anything other than chicken nuggets shaped like dinosaurs.

Minutes passed with no sign of Herbert and Shane found himself drinking the vile coffee just to pass the time. When he lifted the cup to his lips and found it empty, he'd been waiting more than half an hour.

He let more time pass, absently tapping the cup on the table and watching the hands on the clock over the exit. An hour passed with no sign of Herbert.

The ghost didn't have a watch, but he should have noticed the passage of a second hour. That meant he'd either become remarkably distracted or something had happened.

If Herbert were alive, the possibility of being lost was on the table, but not as a ghost. With the cameo necklace in his pocket, Shane should have stood out like a beacon to Herbert no matter where he was.

Shane scanned the cafeteria as he got up to get more coffee. Cool and casual, he looked from face to face while the cup filled. He settled on a man sitting alone at the first table behind the cashier. Anyone who bought food would walk past him, either on their way back out or to find a seat elsewhere in the room. That was a man who enjoyed people.

He affixed a lid to the coffee and had a sip, scowling at the taste he'd somehow forgotten, and walked to the man at the table.

The stranger wore a hospital ID on a lanyard around his neck and what looked like scrubs at first, but in dark blue. He was an orderly, Shane saw on his ID, not a nurse or a doctor. Like everyone else, he was immersed in his phone, reading an article from a news site with a half-eaten sandwich and chips on a plate in front of him.

"Mind if I sit?" he asked.

The orderly looked up and then glanced around the room at all the empty tables before looking Shane in the eye.

"Help yourself," he said.

Shane sat opposite him, and the man smiled before returning to his phone. He was maybe in his early thirties, and Shane could see several tattoos creeping out from under his collar and sleeves.

"Must be tough working here sometimes, huh?" Shane said, sipping his coffee but keeping the scowl from his face.

"How's that?" the man asked. His ID read "Douglas."

"With all the kids, I mean. Being sick and all. Must get stressful."

"Oh, yes," Douglas agreed. "The way I look at it, though, is that things would be much worse if we weren't here. So, of course, there are bad days. But the good ones really make up for it."

"That's a great attitude to have," Shane said.

Douglas smiled and picked up his sandwich, taking a bite.

"Is your child a patient here?" he asked.

"My nephew Herbert," Shane said. Douglas smiled oddly.

"Herbert. Don't hear that name often."

"Sister named him after our grandfather," Shane said.

"Is he doing well, or...?"

"Touch and go," Shane said. "I only got here a little while ago, so I'm not sure what's happening yet. Waiting until, you know, things have settled a little. Thought I'd grab a coffee."

"Of course, yeah," Douglas said.

"Have you worked here long?" Shane asked, smiling over his coffee. This would have been so much more efficient if he'd found a ghost. Small talk was a lot less deceptive with them.

"Four years," Douglas answered.

"Oh wow. How old is the hospital? Looks like a wartime relic or something."

"Almost. Think it was built in 1947," Douglas said, taking a sip from a bottle of water. "Don't quote me on that, though."

"It's practically an antique. These walls must have seen some things, huh?" Shane said.

"For sure. There was a big renovation in the late nineties, but you can still find a lot of the old hospital in the south wing. They closed off a lot of the lower levels and built on top of it. Used to give tours until it was deemed unsafe."

"Oh, yeah? Must have been fun."

"I went on one when I was in high school. It was kind of cool. Old morgue, boiler, file storage. Scary stuff, to be honest. Like haunted house stuff."

Shane chuckled and nodded, trying the coffee again.

"Oh man, don't let my sister hear you say anything about this place being haunted. Bad enough what the kid was saying earlier," he said.

Douglas looked confused for a moment and leaned in.

"What do you mean?"

Shane made a dismissive sound and then shrugged.

"Kids, you know? He's scared because of everything that's going on, and he tells me he thinks he saw a ghost in his room earlier by the foot of the bed."

Douglas grinned and nodded knowingly, eating one of the potato chips on his plate.

"You have no idea, the stories around here. I've worked in pretty much every department. Wherever I'm needed, right? I swear, every department, every floor of this place, has its own ghost story. You can imagine, being around since the forties. We're not supposed to talk about it around the patients, though."

Douglas pushed his plate toward Shane and nodded at it. Shane took a chip and nodded back.

"Probably just overheard something. He can be a little sneaky; I'll give him that. He said the ghost was a doctor, not a patient, so I figure that sounded a little off, anyway. Why would a ghost be a doctor in a hospital, right?"

He chuckled and watched Douglas' reaction. The man's smile came quickly as his eyes lit up.

"He's in osteo, right? Seventh floor?" Douglas asked.

"You got it," Shane said enthusiastically.

"Yeah, I've heard that, too. Dr. Shakes, they call him sometimes? Dr. Death's popular, too. Supposedly a surgeon who had a heart attack in the middle of a surgery, died on the spot."

Shane's eyes widened, and he put on his best smile.

"That is a heck of a back story," he said. After a second, he leaned in and lowered his voice. "You ever seen him?"

Douglas chuckled and shook his head.

"Nah, no. Never seen any of the so-called ghosts. And I'll tell you what, I even Googled that one and nothing. No record of a doctor ever keeling over mid-surgery. You tell your nephew none of that stuff is real. Just people telling stories."

Shane took another drink from his coffee and then pretended to check his watch.

"Listen, I will do that, and I thank you for letting me know. I have to go see if they need anything, though. You have a good day."

"You too. I hope your nephew gets better soon," Douglas said. Shane nodded and waved as he tossed half a coffee in the trash on the way out.

It was time to go to the seventh floor.

Chapter 11
Dr. Death

Shane shared the elevator to the seventh floor with a couple talking about their child's cancer diagnosis. He heard what they were saying, talking in that hushed way people sometimes do in public when they don't want to be overheard but can't possibly think they're not being overheard.

They were young parents, and it was clear the child was their first. Their voices were tired. They looked tired and carried themselves like tired people. Even standing next to one another, whispering as they were, it would not have been out of place for either of them to lean on the wall, close their eyes, and sleep standing up.

This was what Lisette had come for. Not the children, whom she had decided in her perverse mind that she might protect, but these parents. These people were extensions of the people of Burkitt. People she blamed for the pain she felt, the pain that had turned her into a monster.

Tillman Children's Hospital would be full of people like these parents. They would go in and out of the front doors all day long, all week long, for as long as the hospital was in operation. People with sick, injured, and dying children.

Lisette had killed the entire staff of the carnival, and if she had come to the hospital, Shane could see no reason she would not repeat herself. And the "if" was becoming less of a question in his mind.

Something was off about the hospital: missing ghosts. There should have been more around. Herbert missing for so long confirmed it. There was no reason. Herbert had to have discovered something.

The elevator dinged, and a soft, pleasant voice informed them they had reached the seventh floor. The quiet parents got out first and headed to the left. Shane followed them, unsure of where to go.

He was looking for the ghost of the seventh floor, Dr Death, or whatever his name was. Most hospital ghosts were patients. Maybe Shane would have more luck with the fluke of a doctor who had died and come back to haunt his workplace.

Like the other floors he had already visited, the seventh floor was broken into a labyrinth of hallways, closed doors, common areas, and central hubs where doctors and nurses gathered at small, office-like clearings in the maze to run their departments.

The seventh floor featured osteo and bone disease, internal medicine, orthopedics, and nephrology. The parents headed toward osteo and internal medicine, and Shane followed several paces behind. At a branch in the hallway, they continued left toward internal medicine while Shane headed right for osteo, glancing in rooms as he went.

He passed a nurse who smiled, and he nodded but said nothing. He didn't pause at the nurse's station, avoiding eye contact with a woman seated at a computer and a doctor checking over charts.

Shane took the first hallway away from the nurse's station, eager to be out of sight, and made it halfway down the hall before he stopped. A doctor in blood-splattered scrubs stood outside a room, staring into it blankly, perfectly still, and silent.

He was an older man, with gray hair peeking out from under his surgical cap, and more than his fair share of lines creasing his forehead and disappearing behind the mask he wore. He was a ghost.

The rest of the hallway was empty, and Shane started forward once more. He glanced into a few rooms, some of which were occupied by children in bed with legs or arms suspended and rigged with pins and screws and thick casts.

Shane reached the ghost and then turned to glance into the room that had preoccupied him so. It was empty, and the ghost seemed to be just staring out a window at the town visible in the distance, or maybe the cloud-filled sky.

"Everything okay, Doc?" Shane asked quietly.

The ghost turned to Shane and locked eyes with him. There was no moment of recognition there or realization that Shane could see him. The eyes were cold and unfocused, and Shane almost sighed out loud.

He had wanted information from the spirit; a lead on finding Herbert or confirmation that Lisette and Hartwell were in the building. He was rapidly losing hope of that.

"It's time for your surgery," the ghost doctor said, his voice barely registering above a hiss.

The ghost lifted his gloved hand and daintily unhooked the mask from behind his ear. It slipped from his face, dangling from his other ear and exposing a skeletal jaw outlined by bits of flesh that had rotted away.

Shane stared at the ghost, and the ghost stared at him. The moment dragged on and finally Shane did sigh.

"Have you seen the ghost of a man who's about four hundred pounds?" he asked.

"This won't hurt a bit," the surgeon replied. He reached for Shane's throat, his movements slow and methodical.

It had been a good while since Shane had met a ghost that seemed focused on scares rather than harm. This one was probably an absolute nightmare for the kids in the hospital. But he was so slow and intentional that Shane wondered if it was really anything more than a show.

He swatted away the ghost's hands and the doctor seemed to gain focus, his brow knitting in frustration.

"You don't belong here," the ghost spat. He turned quickly and left through a set of double doors. Shane followed him, keeping pace down halls that weaved this way and that, avoiding hospital staff as he kept track of the ghost.

The ghost ducked into a closed room and Shane pretended to check his phone while a janitor made his way down the hall. When no one living was within range, Shane entered the room as well.

The space was a small, windowless operating room. It was not set up for use, and there was very little there besides an operating table, a curtain, and a cabinet, along with the various hookups and outlets needed for power and oxygen and so forth.

"I just need to know if you've seen any new ghosts lately," Shane said, turning a circle. There was a crispness to the air, a chill beyond what was normal with the hospital's air conditioning. The ghost was nearby.

The overhead lights clicked, and the room went dark. Only a narrow pane of glass in the door let in any light from the hall, a thin band that fell on the floor and illuminated nothing but two tiles.

"Other ghost I'm looking for is a woman. She looks like a shadow. You'd remember her if you'd seen her. Might be with a living man."

"You don't belong here."

The voice was a whisper in Shane's ear. The air was cold and smelled like rotten meat mixed with chemicals. It took him a moment to place it. The smell of hospital disinfectants.

Shane turned, but the ghost was not there. He'd done well perfecting his scare technique; Shane was willing to give him that. Staff and patients would have dreaded his presence.

"Tell me what I need to know, and I'll leave," Shane offered.

The light in the window went dark. Shane was unsure if the hall lights had been extinguished or if the ghost had simply obscured the window. Either way, he was plunged into darkness.

A hand fell on Shane's shoulder, squeezing uncomfortably close to his neck.

"You don't—" the ghost began.

Shane took the ghost by the wrist and pulled, lifting his other hand, swiftly taking two of the spirit's gloved fingers, and bending them back as far as they would go. Ghostly bone snapped and the ghost bellowed, yanking away his hand and vanishing into the dark.

"How...?" the ghost demanded. The operating room might have been the one the ghost died in, if Douglas' story was correct. He could have haunted this part of the hospital for decades, which meant he was very comfortable with the area.

At a certain point, a haunting grew bigger than the ghost. Even Shane's home in Nashua suffered the same fate, like the house became a part of its haunting. The floor plan could change; rooms and even floors could appear and disappear. The ghost doctor seemed to enjoy something similar in his little corner of the hospital. It would make fighting him harder until he fully presented himself.

The room grew colder. Shane flexed his fingers and resisted the urge to light a cigarette.

"All you had to do was answer a question," he pointed out.

The ghost remained silent, but air shifted in the room. He could feel faint hints of cool air slashing at his face as though things were rushing past him in the darkness.

A light clicked on, and it was far from Shane. The room had not been that large before. It was a lamp on a bendable arm, a spotlight positioned over an operating table. The light flickered and buzzed, and when it came on again, both it and the table were closer to Shane.

"It's time for your operation," the doctor's voice whispered.

The lights flickered again. The table was in front of Shane now and the light turned toward his face, blinding him.

A shadow crossed his field of vision and he stumbled, avoiding what felt like a strike, as cold air rushed inches from his face. The light strobed, and it was impossible to focus. He was no longer sure which way he faced or where the door was. There was only the surrounding darkness and the impossibly bright white light flashing rapidly in his eyes.

"The only option left is vivisection, I'm afraid," the ghost said.

Shane heard something rattle, metal on metal. An aluminum table covered by a green cloth and full of surgical implements came to rest below the light. Scalpels, saws, scissors, and more things Shane couldn't focus on in the bright light were jumbled together. At first, they appeared brand-new and pristine. They changed as the light flashed, aging and growing rusty, encrusted with old blood and bits of hair-covered meat.

Shane raised an arm and stepped back. A flash of silver glinted in the light and pain seared into the muscle below his wrist. His flesh split along the blade of a scalpel. He cursed but instead of backing away, he moved forward.

In the flashing lights, he could see blood smears across the walls and tattered green curtains. Some were sprays, as though arteries had been severed. Others were blood slashes and handprints, as though someone had climbed to the ceiling.

The doctor raised his arm, scalpel ready to slash again. Shane took his wrist for a second time and pulled him forward. The ghost was not expecting a counterattack even after Shane had broken his fingers. He was either too arrogant or too far gone to understand the situation. Whatever the case, Shane drew him off-balance with a single pull and then drove the heel of his free palm into the ghost's elbow.

The arm snapped like dry wood and the surgeon cried out in surprise. Shane did not relent, sending him to the ground with a knee to the ghost's leg as he was spun backward by his broken arm.

"You have one chance left. Have you seen the shadow ghost?" Shane asked, kneeling next to the doctor, clutching his head firmly, and forcing it down to the tile floor.

"You don't belong—"

Shane squeezed his hands and pushed down at the same time. The ghost's head crunched and then buckled, collapsing in his grip. He felt the force slam against him like a fist, eliciting a grunt between clenched teeth as his muscles tensed and then finally relaxed.

The overhead light buzzed back on, and the room was small once more. Nothing was disturbed, but there were no surgical implements. The only blood was a small group of drops on the floor from the wound on Shane's arm. The cut was shallow, but it was long and bled freely.

He went to the cabinet and searched drawers until he found a roll of surgical tape and gauze pads. It was awkward patching his forearm with just one free hand to hold everything straight, but he staunched the bleeding, and it would do well enough.

The ghost had been a waste of his time, but its presence confirmed his belief that the hospital was haunted, as any hospital should have been. Douglas had said nearly every floor and department had its own ghost stories.

There had to be others, he just didn't know if he had the time to find one willing to talk.

CHAPTER 12
DESPERATE TIMES

It was five minutes before Shane found another janitor. The man was mopping something off the floor in a patient room. Shane walked by the room and then paused outside, pretending to talk on his phone.

Shane walked toward the janitor, head down and pretending to be distracted.

He walked into the janitor, nearly pushing the man down and knocking cleaning supplies from his cart. Immediately apologetic, he helped the janitor right himself and keep the cart steady.

"I'm so sorry, I was just... things aren't good. I should have been watching what I was doing," Shane said, trying to look distraught and contrite as he held the man by the shoulders.

"It's fine. It's okay," the janitor said, uncomfortable by Shane's closeness and by nearly being laid out.

"Let me help you get this cleaned up," Shane offered, picking up a bottle of cleaner.

"It's fine, really," the janitor replied. He was about Shane's age, and his patience was wearing thin. Shane nodded and took a step back.

"Okay, yeah. Again, I'm really sorry."

"Don't worry about it," the other man said. "Have a good day."

Shane nodded and stepped away, circling the cart as the janitor finished tidying up. He had not noticed Shane unclipping his ID badge from the breast pocket of his jumpsuit or slipping it behind the cell phone in his hand.

Shane returned to the elevator and headed down, clipping the other man's ID to his pocket. As long as no one looked at it closely enough to realize he looked nothing like the man in the photo, no one would question him wandering the halls.

Herbert had been tasked with going to the limited-access places in the hospital, but since that hadn't worked out, Shane would have to take up the slack. The morgue was probably his best bet.

Most hospitals kept the morgue in the bowels of the building. Sometimes, they were down next to the kitchens where the patients' meals were cooked, just for convenience's sake. The plumbing and wiring were often complementary to both facilities, so it made sense to have them close.

No one wanted anyone stumbling on the morgue by accident for several reasons, so keeping them in restricted areas was standard procedure. The upside to that was that they were also in out-of-the-way areas with little foot traffic or security. The odds of anyone catching Shane trying to slip in were lower than they were if he was trying to get into the diagnostic labs, for instance.

He got off the elevator in the basement and headed down an unlabeled hallway. Rooms bore names that were just numbers prefaced with the letter B, and anyone down there would have to know where they were going and why.

Traffic was sparse in the basement. Shane passed an orderly and some food service workers. No one spared him a second glance; the ID card pinned to his pocket was a shield against scrutiny.

At the end of the hall, Shane found a sign directing him to what he was looking for. He followed the room numbers down a series of left and right turns, zigzagging through the buzzing fluorescent lights until he found a room with a small plaque on the door that read "Morgue".

There was only one door left at the end of the hall beyond the morgue, a service elevator with big green doors that must have gone to the rear of the hospital and out of sight of most patients, probably set up to head out to a parking lot to allow easy transfer of bodies to funeral homes and mortuaries.

Shane pulled the door to the morgue and it clicked, holding fast. The room was locked, and he frowned. It wasn't the heaviest door he'd seen, and he could probably kick it in, but that might draw attention.

After a moment of thought, his eyes fell on a scanner attached to the wall. He pulled the ID off his shirt and pressed it to the pad. The red light switched to green, and the latch in the door clicked. He pulled it open and went inside.

Automatic lights clicked on, illuminating a large, open space. The tiles were off-white and covered the floors and walls. Only the far wall stood out as different, covered in stainless steel drawers for body storage.

The small office held a desk, a computer, and several cabinets but was otherwise empty. No one was working just then, and there were no ghosts.

Shane walked deeper into the room. A pair of stainless-steel gurneys were pushed to the far wall, empty and pristine. The room was cleaned and neatly organized.

The lights buzzed and clicked off. The sudden switch to black took his eyes a moment to adjust. Soon enough, the faint light from electronics and signs allowed him to have a general sense of the room once more.

He could have moved, of course. The lights were motion-activated and would come on once more if he waved an arm or took a step. But he was curious.

Shane stood in the dark and did nothing. A clock over the office wall noisily ticked away seconds and he counted along in his head. Two minutes passed before someone crept from one of the wall cabinets.

The door had not opened. The body that appeared simply oozed through the wall, slipping soundlessly into the room. It was a boy, maybe eight or nine years old, wearing a hospital gown tied in the back. The front was covered in vomit, dried and crusty in the poor light. His eyes were sunken, and even in the dimness, Shane could see he was pale. The expression "white as a ghost" was not without its merits.

"Hello," he said. The ghost boy was startled and froze in place. His black eyes were wide, and his hands shook.

"I was going!" he blurted out, shaking his head. Shane lifted his hand, and the lights clicked back on.

"You're going where?" he asked. The boy stepped back to the wall, his eyes darting left and right.

"I was going to do it, I was. I just forgot. I was confused—"

"Kid," Shane interrupted. "Whoever you think I am and whatever you think I want, you got it wrong."

The boy shut his mouth and sized up Shane in silence.

"My name's Shane. I just wanted to ask you some questions."

"I don't know anything," the ghost replied quickly.

"Okay, well, you have to know what you were talking about a second ago. What was that about?"

"Nothing," the boy answered.

"Right. Can you tell me where everyone else is?"

They stared at each other. The ghost was thin and looked waxy. His ribs and collarbone were prominent at the top of his hospital gown, and his arms had barely any muscle mass.

"Who?" the boy asked suspiciously.

"You tell me. You can't be the only ghost in this hospital."

The boy shook his head and backed up again until he was nearly against the wall.

"I told you I'll go. I promise. I'll go down there right now."

He was pleading with Shane, and there was fear in his voice. Though he wasn't sure what the boy was talking about, it was more progress than he'd made with the doctor.

Shane stepped toward him and the ghost turned and fled, passing through the wall in the corner. Shane grunted, throwing up his arms in frustration.

"Great," he muttered.

The boy had referenced going down somewhere, which was at least a clue. Douglas had said they renovated the hospital and built over older parts. Maybe there was a floor below them. But the elevator did not go down any farther, and that meant he'd need another method of descent. With Herbert's help, he could cut down the search time dramatically.

Shane reached into his pocket and pulled out the small cameo necklace. In the woods, he planned to put distance between himself and the ghost, to run a mile and force Herbert to come back to the necklace. He couldn't afford to run for a mile now, though.

If he couldn't leave, then he needed Herbert to return to him. If no one was hitting him with iron bars, Shane would have to improvise.

He left the morgue and made his way back to the elevator, walking with purpose but trying to keep the casual look of someone who was supposed to be there.

There was no way to know what kind of clock he was working with. Herbert was missing for unknown reasons. Shane had stolen a hospital ID and a car, both of which someone would eventually come looking for. Then there was the APB that had to be out on him. All it would take was one police officer in a hallway glancing at him for too long and thinking he looked familiar.

He still didn't know if Lisette was in the hospital. Shane's gut told him he was right, though. And the ghost of the boy, the location, everything was sending up signals that set him on edge.

When Shane made it back to the cafeteria, Douglas was gone and new people sat at various tables. Shane grabbed an empty cardboard coffee cup and walked to a table full of condiments, plastic utensils, and napkins.

There was no saltshaker, just a plastic tub full of tiny paper salt packets. He grabbed a handful and tore them open one at a time, dumping the contents into the cup until a couple of inches of crystals covered the bottom.

After glancing around the room to see if anyone was paying attention, he sat in the corner by a soda machine, pulled the cameo necklace from his pocket, and dropped it in the cup. He gave it a quick shake and watched the necklace vanish in the salt.

He then dumped the cup's contents on the table. Herbert appeared before him on the opposite side, behind a chair. They stared at each other, and it took the ghost a beat to realize what happened.

"Shane," he said loudly.

"Herbert," he replied, much more quietly. The ghost turned and looked around the room.

"Oh no. No, you shouldn't have done that," the ghost said. He raised a hand to his head and held it there as he looked around the cafeteria once more.

"Where have you been?" Shane asked.

Herbert shook his head, one hand still sitting on top of it like a hat.

"Come with me," he said, leaving. Shane was forced to follow or lose him again, leaving his spilled salt everywhere but snatching up the cameo and slipping it back into his pocket.

Herbert headed down a hallway away from the cafeteria and toward the elevators.

"You want to tell me what the hell happened?" Shane asked, catching up.

"There are ghosts in the basement. Well, more of a sub-basement. It's sealed off from the rest of the hospital."

"They renovated and built over older parts," Shane explained.

"Sure, yes. There's a boiler room down there, and they have a woman trapped."

"Do you know who it is?"

They reached the elevator, and Herbert nodded to it.

"We need to go to the first floor," he said.

"Not the basement?"

Herbert shook his head.

"First floor. The basement isn't connected."

Shane pressed the button, and they waited for the car to arrive.

"Did you find Lisette?" Shane asked.

"It's children," the ghost said, whispering for no reason. "Lots of them. I don't know who the woman is, but they will kill her. I was trying to prevent them from hurting her when you pulled me back. We have to be quick."

"As quick as we can," Shane assured him. "Why are they doing this?"

The elevator arrived. A woman and a young girl were in it and Shane paused briefly before getting on. Herbert piled in, unseen by the other two passengers. Shane pressed the button for the first floor.

"They're ghosts of children," Herbert said. "Patients from the hospital. There's so many of them, Shane. They're all down there."

Shane stared forward and said nothing. The elevator stopped on the next floor and a doctor got on. He passed right into Herbert's colossal frame and shuddered, feeling the chill of the spirit but not realizing what it was.

"I didn't find Lisette. I don't know if she's here; I didn't have time to look. They're going to kill this woman. I couldn't get them to explain why; it was all I could do to hold them off as long as I did. They're... I can't even explain it. They're so angry, all of them."

CHAPTER 13
THE KIDS IN THE DARK

Shane got off on the first floor and waited for Herbert to show him the way to the mystery sub-basement. Herbert led them past some administrative offices and to a stairwell, and they descended poorly lit stairs that echoed with every single step.

"We need to find Lisette," Shane said. He wasn't arguing that a sub-basement full of murderous ghost children was noteworthy, but it was not the mission.

"That woman could already be dead," Herbert said, his voice raised and nearly frantic. "We have to help her."

"You don't even know who she is, or what she did—"

"It doesn't matter!" Herbert shouted, rounding on him. The stairwell lights flickered, and the temperature dropped to almost freezing. Shane's breath puffed before him in a cloud and then vanished as the lights brightened and the temperature rose.

Herbert covered his mouth with his hand. He stared at Shane, and for a moment, Shane feared the ghost was about to break into tears.

"I'm so sorry," he blurted, looking down.

"It's fine," Shane replied. "I get it."

"No, it's not fine. You're right; we're supposed to be doing a job. We need to do it. It's just... I don't know." The ghost sighed.

"You want to save someone," Shane said. "I understand that. When you lose everything, sometimes you need to find anything to save when you can. Doesn't matter why. Or who."

"Life should still be worth saving, shouldn't it?" Herbert asked. The sadness in his voice was profound. "Just because we're dead, we shouldn't be monsters. We were alive. We had lives and purpose. That should still be important."

"It is," Shane agreed. He clapped the big man on the shoulder. "So, let's go save a life. Maybe some of these kids can point us toward Lisette while we're at it."

"If she's even been here," Herbert said.

He took the lead once more and Shane followed by his side, into a different basement than the one he had already found. This one had darker tiles, worse lighting, and smelled strangely stale.

"I think she is," he said. "Met a kid earlier who was scared of something. Maybe your little gathering here. Whatever the case, he was trying to avoid it, and then bolted rather than answer any questions."

They crossed the basement to a steel door that had once been labeled but was now blank.

The door was locked and didn't have key card access like the morgue. Herbert entered and unlocked the door from the other side, allowing Shane to pull it open.

Herbert had not noticed the smell because of his inability to do such a thing, but Shane was not immune. The sub-basement was foul. A stagnant and moldy stench came up the dark stairs from whatever waited beneath them. It smelled old and forgotten, and the air was humid.

If there were lights, they were controlled elsewhere. Shane followed Herbert down old, cement stairs slick with moisture and pulled out his phone. The flashlight beam illuminated the space directly ahead, showing off mildew-stained cement walls and glistening gray steps down to a tiny vestibule and another sealed door.

"I hope we're not too late," Herbert whispered. He unlocked the next door and Shane entered a hallway lined with overhead pipes and industrial light cages.

Lines had been painted on the floor, mostly vanished now under mildew and puddles fed by myriad constant drips from the pipes. The air was hot and felt thick, and Shane felt the moisture clinging to his face.

"There's a plumber somewhere who needs to be fired," Shane said. Herbert didn't reply; he was already leading them down the damp hall.

Shane's flashlight beam illuminated puddles big and small and the odd pile of sodden refuse that had been left behind when the hospital sealed off the basement. A pair of rats squealed when the light hit them and ran for a hole chewed through solid cement into another room.

Herbert stopped outside of a large steel door that still bore the rusty sign plate of "Boiler Room". None of the pipes went to the room any longer; instead, they passed down to the end of the hallway and into a wall, heading to parts unknown and back to the used part of the building.

"How many are in here?" Shane asked. Herbert shook his head.

"I saw at least a dozen," he answered. "But they didn't all want to be seen. I was mostly focused on trying to keep them from the woman."

Shane breathed deep the hot, unpleasant air. Twelve ghost children was not an easy fight if it came to that. Children were sometimes worse than adults when they were enraged. He hoped Herbert had kept them calm.

He pulled open the door. The air was colder in the boiler room, which was a welcome change. But the darkness was all-encompassing.

Shane swept his flashlight right and then left. There were rusted-out hulks of old machines, disconnected pipes, and piles of junk all over. The floor was saturated in that room as well, and Shane walked through a pool at least an inch deep, growing deeper where mysterious dips in the cement floor appeared at irregular intervals.

Herbert made no noise, but Shane could not avoid splashing. The big ghost led him to the left and then stopped, looking at something Shane could not see. His shoes splashed, and the noise seemed impossibly loud as he came to the ghost's side.

Shane raised his light. A woman sat against the wall on a rusted-out chair, her head flopped to one side. Her face, neck. and arms were marred by dark bruises. He could not tell if she was still alive.

A more immediate concern was that none of the ghosts Herbert had warned him about were visible. Shane swept his light back and forth. Flickers of motion danced at the edges of the beam. Nothing at first, then little more than shadows. Finally, as he approached the woman, the light caught something behind an old furnace. A face, dark as the mold on the walls, with two eyes that gleamed in the light like a cat's. It vanished as soon as Shane could focus on it.

Something splashed behind him, and he turned, catching nothing in the light. A second splash elsewhere and all he caught was the motion of the water, rings spreading from something unseen that had disturbed the surface.

"Think we're late to the party," Shane said.

The woman was a nurse, her ID hanging from the collar of her shirt. Shane approached her carefully. She was about his age and her hair was pulled into a tight bun. This close, he could see that the marks on her were more than bruises. They were patches of frost-bitten flesh. Not as dark and deep as the wounds Lisette left on her victims, which were little more than burns. But they would have been painful.

He reached out, placing a hand on her neck to find a pulse. The body shifted and something plopped to the floor. The sound had a strange softness to it and Shane looked down. The woman's shirt was saturated red, and from underneath, her insides spilled out, landing in a pile at her feet.

"No," Herbert said, his whisper barely a sound. Shane stared at the organs, intestines, and more slowly sliding away from one another in the dampness. He took a step back, to prevent anything from touching his shoes.

"I tried to help her," Herbert said. "I tried. They were listening to me."

"I know," Shane told him. *Maybe* if he hadn't drawn his friend back, he could have saved the nurse. Although Shane thought it was more likely that they would have eventually murdered her in front of Herbert.

The ghost in the morgue made it clear that someone wanted the children down there. Douglas spoke of the hauntings as isolated, every floor with its own story. Someone had pulled everyone together.

Water splashed again. Shane didn't bother turning his light to face it.

"We should go," he told Herbert. The big ghost looked devastated.

"We can't leave her here," he said.

"We won't," Shane told him. "But we have to for now."

"I don't know if I can keep doing this, Shane. I can't keep watching people die. That's not who I am."

"That's not who anyone is, Herbert," Shane pointed out. "But who you are is directly related to how you deal with that. And we need to leave this place before it happens again."

Shane wanted to find Lisette; that hadn't changed. But he could not hope to take on that ghost alongside a dozen homicidal child spirits. He would end up gutted and forgotten in the basement alongside the nurse.

Giggling from the shadows made Herbert turn his attention away from the dead woman.

"You don't have to do this," he said to the darkness.

The response was more laughter, like a distant echo. It came from nowhere and everywhere. Shane felt his jaw tighten. If they were working together, it would be much more difficult to handle them. It would be like the dark ones in his cellar, things that were more dangerous as a group than as individuals. That was true of many predators.

"How are your eyes down here?" Shane asked.

"I see everything," Herbert answered.

"Good. You cover our six."

He turned the light from his phone back in the direction they had come. A hint of movement skittered just out of the edge of the beam. He ignored it, heading forward through the puddles. Herbert was at his heels, not speaking a word. Shane had to trust he could handle the job of getting them out safely.

They reached the spot where Herbert had first stopped and observed the woman in the chair, and Shane paused. The way back was no longer the way back at all. The waterlogged passage stretched on past machines and pipes that had not existed on their first walk.

More pipes dripped and steam hissed from valves. Shane cursed and looked in the other direction. More fleeting bits of movement, shadows like cockroaches avoiding the light. On the ceiling, hidden among the pipes, a pair of eyes like golden fire blinked and then vanished.

"What have they done?" Herbert whispered.

"It's a trap," Shane answered. "Old haunted house trick. More ghosts means it's a little more complex. If they've been here a long time, they can make it very effective."

"It looks real, though. It's not real, is it?"

"Real as a ghost," Shane explained.

Whether an exit was hidden from them didn't matter. They would need to find the way out if they wanted to leave, and doing so was not going to be easy. And his life was at risk. So was Herbert's. They couldn't kill him in the traditional sense, but they could destroy him.

"How do we get out?" Herbert asked quietly.

"Any way we can. If we don't get out, then, well, we'll never get out."

The statement sounded foolishly redundant, but he trusted Herbert understood the meaning. The children were not playing games. They were out for blood, and someone had tipped them in that direction. There was no way so many ghosts with murderous intent could have been in the hospital all this time with the hospital still operating like it should.

People found reasons to both explain and avoid haunted places. They blamed things like gas leaks, poor construction, bad luck, and anything under the sun. People died or went missing, and slowly, everyone else would realize a place was bad.

At a hospital, patients would stop going. They'd travel farther to get care somewhere else. Employees would quit. Services would get cut back, and eventually, the place would close. It would seem organic. No one would ever seriously blame it on ghosts. Red tape and funding would be blamed. Anything other than the truth.

If Tillman Children's Hospital was dangerously haunted by killer spirits, that was what would have happened, and it would have happened years ago. Something else was inspiring the ghosts of those children, and it was all the confirmation Shane needed.

Lisette was there. He knew it.

He needed to survive long enough to find and stop her.

CHAPTER 14
PREDATOR AND PREY

The sound of children singing echoed down the halls above the sound of hissing steam and dripping water. It sounded far away, and as though it were coming from some place deep in a hole or cave. Shane couldn't make out any words, just the sing-song voices.

He headed in the direction he was sure they had initially come. When he reached the spot where the door should have been, there was only a cement wall holding up rusted and rickety pipes. He pressed his hand to it and felt the dampness and spongy mold.

Something splashed loudly ahead of them. The beam of the phone light whipped toward it as Shane searched the area. He could only see the ripples in the water.

"Anything?" he asked.

"Shadows," Herbert answered softly. "Shapes. Always out of the corner of my eyes. A lot of them."

"Just keep your eyes open. Ghosts don't usually haunt other ghosts. They shouldn't be able to get close without you noticing."

"Shouldn't, yeah."

Shane led them onward. Water splashed loudly, and he felt deep cold seeping into his foot. It was growing deeper, the level rising to the tops of his boots. The air remained hot, cloying even, thanks to the steam, but the water below was almost deathly cold.

Herbert was unaffected and hadn't noticed the change but the farther they traveled, the deeper it got. As it rose to his shins, Shane stopped and looked back. Going further put him at risk. He expected something to pull him under, sooner rather than later.

"Double back," Shane said.

"Why?" Herbert asked.

Shane flashed the light down quickly, and the ghost nodded.

"It wasn't anywhere near this deep before," Herbert pointed out. Shane chuckled humorlessly.

"No, it wasn't."

Herbert was getting a crash course in hauntings and what other ghosts—malevolent ones—excelled at. His afterlife had been strangely sheltered. He was lucky.

They headed back the way they had come and though it was subtle, the ghosts had changed the hallway again. The path to the dead nurse had vanished. There were no longer branches along the route.

Water sloshed around Shane's legs as he forced his way forward. It was up to his knees now. There was no longer an option to head to shallower ground.

Rats squealed and ran along the exposed pipes on the walls. Some would dart left or right, vanishing into narrow openings alongside the pipes and when Shane's light swept across them, he'd see larger movement, ghosts hiding in the deepest of the shadows, their eyes glinting in the light for only a moment.

The water was dark, and an oily film sat atop it. The smell reminded Shane of an old pond, stagnant in the heat of summer after most of the water evaporated and left only sludge and decaying matter behind.

Shane stopped when it was waist-deep, leaning against the wall with his elbow on a rusty pipe.

"What are you doing?" Herbert asked.

Shane reached into his pocket and pulled out a cigarette, using it to gesture around.

"Seems like time for a break," he said.

"We need to keep moving. *You* need to keep moving."

Shane lit the cigarette and shook his head. Splashes in the distance sounded over faint whispers and the distant, singsong-y recitation of a nursery rhyme. He took a puff and exhaled.

"I think we should wait here."

"For what?" Herbert said. He was anxious and it showed, while Shane felt the opposite.

"There will be more of the same if we keep walking. Maybe I fall into a sinkhole. Maybe a ghost pulls me under. I don't want to get my cigarettes wet. Let's just wait."

"Shane…" Herbert scoffed.

He nodded to the ghost, cigarette clutched loosely between his lips, and put away his lighter.

"Kids are impatient," he assured the ghost. "You'll see."

He wasn't positive his approach would work, but he believed that the ghosts of children often had impulse-control issues. Eloise, for instance, would not stand for him just waiting there and wasting time. With at least a dozen ghosts, one or two were bound to lash out.

They stood together, Shane half-soaked, and waited. Herbert scanned the darkness back and forth, up and down the length of the flooded hallway. Shane smoked and did nothing.

The singing and whispers faded to silence. Soon, they could hear only dripping water and hissing steam. Shane endured the curious discomfort of his lower half freezing while the upper half was steamed and sweaty.

In time, the dripping water and hissing steam faded to silence as well. Then, there was nothing at all. Shane drew in a long breath and glanced at Herbert. The big ghost held his eye. Neither of them said anything.

The faint sound of ripples in the water caused them to turn. It wasn't a splash. It sounded more like something slipping from a tunnel, low and slow, into the water, like a gator entering a river from shore.

Shane held his phone up and focused on something floating toward them. He couldn't tell what it was. Even in the light, most of the shape seemed to be immersed, hidden below the dark surface. Something was floating toward them, only bits of it buoyant enough to rise to the top. Undefined shapes, little bulges and peaks. And hair. Shane could see hair.

The body of the nurse floated toward him, face-down in the water. The back of her head breached the surface and rumpled bits of her clothing rose above the water while most stayed just below the surface.

The body rotated slowly as it reached Shane. A shoulder came up and rolled back under. Her pale face appeared, plastered with hair that obscured most of her features, and then her blood-soaked shirt, now diluted to a pale pinkish red because of the water.

She stopped, bobbing in place, her head less than a foot from Shane and Herbert. The big ghost averted his eyes while Shane took a long draw from his cigarette and waited.

"Shane," Herbert whispered. It was the only sound in the hallway.

"Shhh," Shane replied, drawing it out like a snake slithering through dry leaves. He adjusted the cigarette between his lips, the dampness of them from the steam sticking to the paper of the filter and almost gluing it in place.

The water grew colder. He could feel it soak into his legs, chilling him deeply. His pulse quickened, an involuntary reaction to the influx of cold. He tensed his hands and then balled them into fists.

The body of the nurse bobbed, the water disrupted by an unseen force. It lapped at the sides of her bloodless cheeks, pulling at the loose hair and brushing it aside until her face was clear.

Dead, white eyes stared at Shane. He stared back. Somewhere at the end of the hallway, a hiss of steam escaped from a pipe, and the dead woman's lips spread into a smile.

Hands from the pipes pulled Shane against the wall. They pulled at his collar, chest, neck, and arms. Four hands at first and then more. The nurse's corpse rolled again as her hand rose from the water and reached for him. She righted herself and stood, the sound of water pouring from her saturated body filling the narrow space.

Shane struggled against the grip of multiple tiny hands that dug into him like hooks and panic overwhelmed Herbert.

"Stop doing this, please," the ghost begged. "Let him go."

The children ignored Herbert and sank small, freezing fingers into Shane's flesh, puncturing deeply enough to draw blood as he struggled to break free.

"Stop!" Herbert shouted, desperate for them to pay attention.

The dead nurse grasped Shane's face, cradling him in her hands. Oily water flowed from her mouth, over her teeth, and down her front.

"Have you been naughty again?" she asked. Her voice was like the sound of wet heaving.

Shane's wrists were pinned tight to the pipes. He couldn't even free a shoulder to gain leverage. The nurse opened her mouth and Shane snapped his head forward in a quick, blunt strike. His forehead smashed against her nose with a meaty thud. She didn't let go or slow down, despite her nose breaking and flattening to the left side of her face.

"Stop!" Herbert yelled again.

Shane let the ghosts hold him steady and lifted his legs. He kicked out, slamming both heels into the nurse's split-open gut and forcing her back. The unsteady body stumbled and fell, slamming the back of her head against pipes on the other side of the hall.

Someone screamed, but it was not the nurse. A ghost emerged from the murk, a child whose head sat askew on its shoulders. It was a boy, not even ten years old, Shane thought, and his expression showed the rage of a child throwing a tantrum.

"Stop," Herbert told the boy, who paid him no mind. The ghost came at Shane, who raised a foot once more and planted it firmly in the ghost boy's face, knocking him back onto the nurse's corpse.

Shane fell to the floor. It was as though a switch had been turned off. The hands and the water vanished, and they were in the hall as it should have been once more. Damp and hot, but not flooded and no longer endless. The door to leave, the same one through which they'd entered, was only a few yards away.

The nurse was gone, but the boy he'd kicked was in her place. He touched his face where Shane had kicked him and pulled his hand away. He was missing a tooth. The boy probed the spot with his tongue and then stared at Shane in astonishment.

"How did you do that?" he said. Shane got to his feet and shook his arms. He could still feel the tiny puncture wounds up his arms and across his shoulders and torso from the little ghost hands.

"Used my foot," Shane replied. He straightened his jacket and then took a step forward, holding out his hand. The ghost boy stared at it.

"It's okay," Herbert assured the other ghost.

"You're alive," the boy said to Shane.

"In a hurry, too," Shane replied, nodding at his extended hand.

The ghost reached for it tentatively and then took it. Shane pulled him to his feet. Another ghost appeared, still halfway immersed in shadows, and kept her eyes fixed on Shane.

More crept from the darkness, some well into their teens and others far younger. Most wore hospital gowns, but some were in their own clothes. Some bore signs of trauma, and others looked to have succumbed to long bouts with diseases.

"Why did you do it?" Herbert asked, kneeling before the boy. "I thought you were going to let her live."

"No, we weren't," another spirit answered. This was an older girl, maybe in her mid-teens. Her hair was buzzed almost bald, and her limbs were swollen.

"But—"

"She was bad," the boy with the missing tooth said. "She deserved to die."

"Bad how?" Shane asked.

"She killed kids," the buzzed girl answered bluntly. "She'd change medications or give you too much of something."

"Or cover your face," another little girl said.

"Or turn off the machines," added a boy.

Shane looked at Herbert, who was stricken all over again. The nurse was killing patients, and the patients returned for revenge. As good a reason as any for so many ghosts to appear, and to kill.

"Why now, though?" Shane asked. "She must have been doing this for a long time."

"She told us we could fight back," the buzzed girl said.

"The nurse?" Herbert asked, confused. The girl shook her head.

"No. We don't have to hide down here anymore and just watch them hurting everyone else. We won't! This place is supposed to save kids, not hurt them, and we're not going to let them do it anymore."

The girl was angry and rightfully so, Shane thought. But the rhetoric rang a bell, and it was not from the children.

"Shane," Herbert whispered. The air swirled around them like a cold gust on a winter's day. A figure emerged from the door, black cloaked in black. There was no face, barely even a body, but Shane recognized her all the same.

It was Lisette.

CHAPTER 15

PANDEMONIUM

Shane's back hit the ground so hard he felt the wind push from his lungs. He gasped and his cigarette rolled across his face, burning his cheek before it hit the damp ground and extinguished. His phone skittered to the wall, making the beam of light spin around and then settle on the ceiling.

The shadow of Lisette was on top of him in an instant. She felt massive, an unbearable weight forcing him down. All he could see was darkness without form until a hand emerged, blurry around the edges as though viewed through a fog.

She spread her fingers and reached out, ready to grasp Shane's face and sear his flesh with deadly cold. He struggled beneath her while still trying to catch his breath.

With a wordless cry of anger, Herbert barreled into the dark spirit. His immense body was like a freight train, and the shadow ghost was powerless to slow it. He thundered forward, forcing her off Shane and then down the hallway several steps as he wrapped his arms around her form and crashed to the ground on top of her.

Shane scrambled backward, getting to his feet as quickly as he could and breathing deeply, eyes searching the dark for the ghosts. He could hear Herbert growling like an animal and quickly scooped up the phone, directing the beam of light toward the sound.

The big man was on his feet again, and Lisette was with him. Her hands were on his throat, and they moved in a desperate, awkward dance. He would pivot to one side and try to use his bulk to overpower her, and the shadowy form would simply glide with him, using his movements to give her an advantage, keeping him locked in her grip.

Herbert was not a fighter and never would have been. Lisette was at a loss as well since her ability to burn her prey to death would not work on Herbert. She could still do him harm if she could remove his head as she seemed to be trying to do.

The big ghost struggled to speak but could not. Shane was certain his words would be wasted anyway. She would not listen to him, not now or ever again.

They danced toward an old furnace, the fight going back and forth. The ghost children remained in the shadows, some watching with fear in their eyes but others looking excited.

Shane made a beeline for the spirits.

"Herbert, drop," Shane shouted. The big man's eyes focused on him, and to his credit, he didn't hesitate, and immediately collapsed like a sack of potatoes. Shane dropped low and forced his shoulder into Lisette's form, slamming her against the cast-iron furnace door. In an instant, Herbert was free from her grasp and splayed out on the ground. The iron had forced Lisette back to her item, giving them a reprieve.

"She's so strong," Herbert said, finally able to speak.

"I noticed. Let's get going."

Shane slipped a hand into his pocket, sliding an iron ring over his finger as he turned to watch the ghosts of the children congregate around him.

Some stayed in the shadows, and Shane recognized the boy from the morgue. They locked eyes for a moment before the boy ducked into the darkness. Others went with him, but some stayed, like the girl with the buzzed cut. They were eager to continue the fight, even without Lisette to back them.

Wherever the shadow ghost had gone, she would return quickly. Hartwell had to be in the hospital somewhere, keeping her haunted item safe. She could be back in minutes.

"You're like everyone else," the girl told Shane. "No one cared for us. But she does. She wants to protect us."

"She just wants to kill people," Shane pointed out. The ghost's eyes narrowed, and her lips curled into the faintest of smiles.

"Good," she said.

She ran at Shane, snarling like a beast, and he leveled a carefully timed jab into her chin. The iron ring hit against the ghostly flesh for a fraction of a second, and then she was gone.

Those who remained in the hallway were hesitant, but they did not flee. Shane braced himself for another attack when an alarm broke through silence from somewhere above.

"Code Silver to the Pediatric Unit. Code Silver, Pediatric," a muffled voice said over the hospital intercom. The children vanished as though the call had been for them, and Shane was left alone with Herbert.

"What the hell is a code silver?" he asked.

"I don't know," the ghost replied.

Shane knew hospital codes were a secretive way to alert staff to serious issues without scaring patients, but silver was not something he was familiar with. The timing was suspicious if nothing else. In any event, it had drawn away the children and given Shane and Herbert the opportunity they needed.

Herbert followed behind Shane's heels as they left the basement. He was still rattled by the children and his encounter with Lisette, but he would need to get used to it on the go.

Shane pushed open the door to the main floor just as a second alarm went on.

"Code Silver to the ER. Code Silver, ER," the voice said.

A second code in a second place had to be an emergency that wasn't medical. This was not a patient in need of a doctor, it was a security issue.

"The ER is close by," Shane said, weaving through the halls that Herbert had initially led him down. They passed an empty security office and made it to the lobby, where people were in a frenzy. Patients were pushing their way to the front doors while a lone security officer tried to keep everyone calm. No one was able to get free, and panic was becoming anger.

Dozens of families, some with small children in tow, were fighting to get to the door. Just as many people seemed to have no idea what was happening. Outside the hospital, through the glass doors, Shane could see something blocking the exit. Someone had parked a truck outside the doors, preventing them from opening fully.

Shane cut through the crowd toward the hall to the ER. More patients and even staff flooded from the area, some pushing people out of their way and shouting for help.

What the hell is going on, Shane thought, fighting through the crowds. Ahead, in the ER, someone screamed, and a new rush of people appeared. Men, women, and children ran down the hall. Shane pressed against the wall, avoiding the initial rush and then lifting his arms, using his elbows to force people out of his way as he pushed against the flow.

Maybe fifty or more people had forced their way down the hall until they reached the bottleneck of the front doors. They shouted for those ahead to move, some practically hysterical.

Shane reached the ER and found a scene of chaos. Beds were flipped and curtains were torn aside, while medical supplies were scattered from knocked-over tables. Only a few people remained, cowering in corners and huddled with others. Terrified, wide eyes turned to Shane when he entered.

A nurse waved frantically at him, trying to get him to leave or hide, and he simply raised a hand, indicating he had seen her as he continued forward.

A security guard lay face-down on the ground, his gun drawn but unused in his hand. Several feet away, a man lay broken, his arms at odd angles, and a black handprint burned down to the bone of his skull.

Another nurse was checking the man for a pulse and coming up empty. Shane heard a static click and saw a second security guard, ducking behind a desk with more staff and a few patients, whispering into a walkie-talkie. There was no sign of Lisette anywhere, but the damage she had wrought was enough.

People screamed again, the sound coming from the way Shane had come. He turned in time to see a pair of police officers pushing through the panicked crowds. The uniformed men had their weapons drawn, and they immediately focused on Shane, the only person in the room still standing.

One officer branched left, and the other kept his gun trained on Shane. He saw recognition dawn on the man's face and cursed in his head as he raised his hands.

"I just got here," he said.

"Shut up," the officer said, approaching cautiously.

"Jesus, get down!" the security guard yelled, catching sight of the officer and Shane. The cop saw the guard, and his drawn weapon, and changed focus. He held his gun at arm's length and switched from the guard to Shane and back.

"Both of you, hands where I can see them."

"I'm just here checking on my nephew," Shane said, trying to brush off the officer's concerns.

"He's lying," someone yelled. Shane sighed and turned to the source, a nurse he vaguely recognized from his earlier tour of the building. "He's been wandering around here alone for over an hour."

"That a fact?" the officer said. "Thought you looked familiar. You're that guy from the APB."

Shane looked at Herbert.

"What do I do?" the ghost asked.

Shane didn't have much of an answer. Two cops and an armed security guard meant someone would probably get shot if they fought back. He shrugged.

"This might take a minute to figure out," he said.

"Shut up," the cop said again. "Baxter, over here."

The second officer joined his partner, gun still drawn.

"Place is clear; there's no one else. What have you got?"

"APB suspect from earlier. Nurse said he's been wandering the place for hours."

"One hour," Shane corrected.

The officer scoffed and grabbed his wrist to cuff him. Blood ran over Shane's hand from the wounds up his sleeves, and he cringed.

"What the hell is this?" he said, turning over Shane's arm and pulling back his sleeve. The loose bandage came off the scalpel slice, and the many punctures from the fingers of the ghost children looked like a series of evenly spaced holes along his flesh.

"Jesus," the officer said, looking up at Shane.

"Rough day. That's why I'm in the hospital," he explained.

More officers arrived in the room, and those in hiding were coaxed out. Everyone was talking at once, and Shane's arms were pulled behind his back as he was put into handcuffs.

The security officer was first to point out that Shane had not been involved and only showed up after everything was over, but it scored him no points in terms of being freed. Police coordinated a search effort, looking for their active suspect as a third warning came over the intercom.

"Code Silver to Radiology. Code Silver, Radiology," the voice said.

The police were on their radios and scratchy updates came through about a suspect fleeing the scene on foot to the west.

The officer forced Shane onto a bench seat near the ER entrance and called it in over the radio that he had a suspect in custody.

"I can create a distraction," Herbert offered. Shane shook his head.

"I don't have a trick for getting out of cuffs. And we can't leave. This is Lisette," he told the ghost.

"Then what do we do?"

"Go find out what's happening in the Code Silvers. See what Lisette is doing," Shane advised. "Be quick this time, huh?"

"Yeah," Herbert said, trying to sound positive. He left at a run, pushing unseen through the crowds and leaving a chill in his wake.

Shane shifted awkwardly in his seat, trying to get his arms more comfortable as he pondered the next move. He wasn't keen on getting violent with the police, but he wasn't sure there were better options available. If he left the hospital, nothing would prevent Lisette from killing everyone.

Police came and went while the crowds at the exit grew angrier. The main entrances were blocked by vehicles. Tow trucks were inbound, but police were preventing people from heading out emergency exits as the hunt for the mystery attacker continued. No one had a decent description, just someone dressed all in black.

"It was the children," Herbert said, appearing again at Shane's side. "They killed the parents of a child who suffered a heart attack. Something genetic; it wasn't even the parents' fault."

"Lisette doesn't care," Shane said. The officer who had taken him into custody turned around to look at him, radio in hand. Shane smiled.

"Four main exits have cars parked against them. It will be hard to escape," Herbert continued.

"Yup," Shane agreed under his breath, eyeing the officer.

"More police are coming. The FBI agent will be here soon, I bet." Herbert looked around nervously, as though merely mentioning it would conjure the agent out of thin air.

"Uh-huh," Shane muttered. Things were quickly falling apart. "Find the children again. If you held them off as long as you did before, it means they were listening to you. You need to get them to listen again."

"Shane," Herbert said, shaking his head. "You saw what happened. No one listened to me."

"If no one listened, they would have killed her in front of you. They're a group, like you and the others at the carnival. Not everyone will follow Lisette. I don't know how much longer they'll keep me here, so you need to do what you can while you can."

Herbert looked hesitant, and Shane nodded at him.

"You've got this, Herbert. Go."

The ghost nodded and left again. Shane sighed and leaned against the wall, twisting his wrists. The situation was chaotic. Police were securing the hospital department by department as their numbers allowed. They would have to evacuate civilians soon, out of smaller exits or wherever it was safe to do so. They'd take Shane at the same time, back to the local precinct. Herbert would be forced to come with him.

Lisette was proving herself adept at sowing chaos. She could jam up the carnival and now Shane by using murder as a distraction. She knew how to play the living, the law in particular, to keep people who could stop her out of her way.

Minutes passed and Shane could only pick up vague bits of conversation between police and guards and radio communications. The tow trucks arrived, and the truck at the door was being removed. Another Code Silver came over the intercom and everyone was on edge.

"Shane Ryan," a voice said, drawing his attention back to the hall that led from the ER to the blocked main entrance. A man in a suit approached and though they hadn't formally met, Shane recognized him from the road where the carnival had burned. It was Agent Ventura from the FBI.

"My name is Xander Ventura, I'm with the Behavioral Analysis Unit of the FBI. I've been looking forward to speaking with you."

"I bet," Shane replied.

Time was up.

CHAPTER 16
EYES THAT SEE

Ventura escorted Shane to a vacant office down the hallway from the hospital's main lobby. Still cuffed, Shane sat in a chair while the agent sat on the edge of a desk, looking at him as though studying an animal in a zoo.

"What happened?" he asked, gesturing vaguely in Shane's direction. "You look like you've been through the wringer."

"Had a fight with a bunch of homicidal children," Shane told him. Ventura nodded.

"You know, I keep seeing your name come up in my cases lately. You're from Nashua, and that's where you were first questioned about a murder at the Bartolomy and Sons Carnival and Sideshow, is that right?"

"First? I think so," Shane said.

"And then, of course, you went to Connecticut. Talked to a medical examiner there about another murder that was tied to the same carnival."

"Was that a question?"

Ventura smiled and shook his head.

"No, Mr. Ryan. It wasn't."

Ventura's eyes were keen. He seemed like he was playing a character when he spoke to Shane, like he was trying to show off his knowledge and maybe somehow put Shane on the defensive. That he could see ghosts was not something Ventura was sharing, and Shane wondered how much it had influenced the agent's decision to pursue the carnival case or to go looking into Shane's past.

"Now, I could tell you about the hardware store you visited that was owned by two other victims, or abandoning a pickup truck owned by a retired carnival performer, or even witnesses seeing you on the steps of a burning courthouse where a judge was found murdered, but I don't know that me telling you any of that would surprise you."

"Not really, no," Shane said. "I was there when it all happened, so, you know. Firsthand knowledge."

"Right, yes. Of course. Can I ask you something else?"

"Floor is yours, Agent," Shane said.

"What is the Iron Tournament?"

The question caught Shane off-guard. The Iron Tournament was an underground fighting competition between the living and the dead that Shane had been forced to enter in Boston. It led him to discover a dangerous and ancient ghost named Lazarus who proved to be far more than he had seemed.

"I have to assume—since you're asking—that you already know," Shane replied.

"Sure," Ventura said. "And the Cult of the Endless Night? Can you offer any insight into them?"

Ventura was good. He had done homework Shane was not sure anyone could. The cult was powerful, and if it still existed in any realistic form, it would be made up of secretive billionaires who trafficked in ghosts as collector's items and assassins and spies. Shane had mostly put an end to it with an explosion inside a defunct army base inside a mountain.

Shane leaned forward.

"What made you realize that Herbert was dead when you saw him on the street earlier?" he asked.

Now it was Ventura's turn to be caught off-guard. The agent's back stiffened and his mouth twitched, lips pursing, as he considered a reply.

"Herbert. That was the… larger man?"

"Called him The Thousand-Pound Man in the carnival, but that was a bit of showbiz, I think. He was never that big," Shane pointed out.

"You were at the carnival when it burned," Ventura said. It was not a question, but Shane shook his head.

"We were not."

"I've already sent prints to the lab for analysis. I know you were driving the truck."

"Never denied that. But the carnival was torched before we got there."

He was avoiding the issue of Herbert, ignoring Shane's question, and sticking to the details of the crimes.

"Convenient," Ventura answered.

"Not in the slightest. There were a lot of innocent people there."

"Yes. Among the dozens of murders I can link you to in the past several weeks. I have other cases in Detroit, in New Orleans, in Boston, in New York, hell, even in Canada. You're there for all of them, and when you leave, there are dead bodies on the ground. More than a hundred of them in the past five years. But you survive, Mr. Ryan. Every time."

"Call me lucky," he said. Ventura didn't smile.

"Are you a serial killer, Mr. Ryan?"

The question was both forthright and earnest, and Shane had to laugh.

"Is that what you think?"

"It's what I'm asking. A simple yes or no will do for now."

Shane leaned forward again, his eyes narrowed. Still, he could not wipe the smile from his face.

"You never answered my question."

"Which was?"

"What tipped you off about Herbert?"

Ventura inhaled slowly.

Calming breaths, Shane thought. He wanted to stay in control, to lead the conversation. Herbert was outside of that control, part of a different narrative, and he didn't want to walk down that road. Not yet, at least.

"We're talking about you, Mr. Ryan. And your victims."

Shane shook his head. He was getting a feeling off Ventura. More showmanship, or something like it. He was not as confident as he appeared. Certainly not as much as he wanted Shane to believe.

"Who knows that you can see ghosts?"

The agent swallowed hard. Another sharp inhale and he averted his eyes, if only for a moment.

"Mr. Ryan—"

"There's a killer in this hospital right now. It's not me, though. The local cops can attest to that. Someone was murdered while I was in custody. I came here looking for her."

"*Her?*" Ventura asked.

His anxiety evened out. He was good at masking it, but not perfect. Shane wondered if he had a lot of field experience. He was confident when he stayed on task and topic. But he didn't like curveballs. And he definitely didn't like ghost talk. Shane understood. If it was new, something he was still adjusting to, then even he didn't know how he felt about it, let alone others. Shane was certain it was a secret he kept from everyone.

"Her name is Lisette. She was a part of the Bartolomy carnival decades ago."

"Decades?" Ventura said. He pulled out a small notepad and wrote something in it.

"Decades. Her son was the Alligator Boy in the freakshow. He was murdered in a town called Burkitt. I'm guessing you found that place in your research."

"The judge and some of the other victims—"

"All of them," Shane corrected. "All originally from Burkitt."

"They were involved in the death of this woman's son?"

"Yeah. They tore him apart."

"Okay. Then why would she be here?"

"Lost herself in vengeance. She killed everyone in the carnival and is now on a quest to do for other children what she couldn't do for her own. Save them from anything she can, at any cost."

Ventura grunted and scribbled more notes.

"And how old is this Lisette now if this is revenge for a decades-old crime?"

"Ghosts don't really age, Ventura," Shane pointed out. The man looked up from his notebook, a strange half-smirk on his face.

"I see. You're pinning this all on a ghost."

"You've seen the faces, right? Handprint, frostbite, burned right down to bone."

"I have," the agent confirmed. There was a lack of understanding in the tone. He was trying to play it cool, but something about his demeanor belied an ignorance that he was trying to brush past.

"Why do you think it gets cold when they're around?"

"Who?" Ventura asked.

"The dead. You can keep playing coy, but I saw you talking to Herbert. It's just us in here. Be honest with me."

"I need *you* to be honest, Ryan."

Shane sighed and leaned back. He kept his eyes on Ventura and shook his head.

"You can play this by the book, and today's going to end with more dead bodies in this hospital. Or you can go with what I know you already know. Have you only been able to see them for a short time?"

"Ryan, I'm not here to answer—"

"People are going to die," Shane interrupted, his voice harsh but quiet. "Is it worth pretending something else is happening? If you don't care about the people dying, why investigate it at all?"

"I care," Ventura said, offended. "I care very much."

"Then stop jerking me around. We're probably the only two people who can end this before it gets worse."

The agent stood and paced the three steps it took to get across the small office. He looked at Shane and pulled his lower lip into his mouth before pushing it back out in a forced exhale.

"It's not new. It's just... I haven't seen many," he said, avoiding eye contact.

"I can think of worse things. There are plenty I wouldn't have seen if I had the choice," Shane replied.

"I thought I was crazy. So did my parents and the doctor they sent me to. I've spent a lot of years wondering if the person I was talking to in any given situation was alive or not. And I haven't brought it up to anyone since I was... maybe fifteen."

"You can't tell?" Shane asked.

"Tell?"

"No, I guess not. I mean, you must be able to tell with some. If they're alive or not."

"I've only seen a few that I know of. I saw a man one time when I was a boy, and I knew..." he paused and took a breath. Shane shifted in his seat and Ventura looked at him as though unsure whether to continue.

"Bad one?" he asked.

"He was torn open. Like something had pulled out his insides," Ventura explained. "First one I ever saw. Knowingly, anyway. I just thought he was a man who'd had a terrible accident. But no one else saw him. No one believed me."

"That's how most people tend to be," Shane said.

"But the man," Ventura continued. "He knew I could see him. And he followed me. For years. He'd died in an accident near the park by my house, and he was always there. In my house, even, until we moved. I went back years later, and he was still there."

"Probably be there forever until you destroy him. Or move him, I guess."

The agent gave Shane a perplexed look.

"You can't destroy him. I tried, believe me. Again and again. He kept coming back."

Now it was Shane's turn to be confused.

"How did you try?"

"Something I discovered when I was going through my training at the FBI. You can use iron as a weapon. I think it stems from folklore. There are stories about fairies and other mythical creatures being allergic to the metal. I've used it to destroy four of them. Five, I suppose, with Herbert, was it? But that ghost in the park always comes back somehow."

Shane laughed, and it was the first solid, deep, belly laugh he'd had in a long time. Ventura's expression transitioned from confused to amused as the contagious nature of laughter took hold of him.

"What's so funny?" he asked.

"That was great, thank you," Shane said, calming down. "Herbert is fine, by the way. Iron doesn't destroy ghosts."

"But I've seen it," Ventura began.

Shane leaned to one side in his chair, showing his hands cuffed behind him.

"See that? Iron ring. Good if you need to knock some sense into a spirit. They don't get destroyed, they get shot back to their haunted item. It's like an instant return-to-sender."

There was a drawn-out silence between them.

"What's a haunted item?" Ventura asked finally.

Someone shouted outside the office, and people ran past. As amusing as it was to talk to someone who seemed to be new to the world of ghosts, they were wasting time they didn't have. Shane needed to convince the man to let him go, or at least help him find Lisette and take her down.

He could see Ventura was torn in two directions. In his mind, the ghost aspect of the case was a separate thing. The agent in him wanted an easy-to-understand explanation. He wanted a killer who could be brought to justice, and Shane fit the bill. It wasn't like he could go to his superiors with tales of a haunted carnival.

"Find me some salt," Shane said.

"What?"

"Get a shaker's worth of salt, and I'll prove that everything I am saying is true."

CHAPTER 17
TRAPPED

"Salt."

Ventura set a handful of salt packets from the cafeteria on the desk in front of Shane.

"Eager to see what happens next," he continued.

"I need my hands," Shane said.

He had thought they were bonding over ghosts, but it was not the case. The agent shook his head.

"Nice try," he said. Shane rolled his eyes.

"Fine. Right front pocket. There's a cameo necklace in there. It's going to be cold."

He leaned back and pushed his hips forward. Ventura frowned at the position he'd put himself in.

"Ryan, what the hell are you doing?"

"You got the salt. Trust me."

"I don't trust you."

"Fine, trust your eyes. I'm handcuffed. Humor me for two minutes. Right front pocket."

Ventura approached him cautiously, drawing his sidearm from a holster under his arm at the last minute. He trained it on Shane with one hand while he reached into his pocket with the other. It was an awkward moment between them, and Shane would have preferred doing this with his own hands, but he was in a tight spot.

The other man struggled to find what he was looking for, but eventually winced and pulled his hand out quickly, taking the necklace with him. He dropped it on the desk next to the salt packets.

"It's freezing," he said.

"They always are. Cover it in salt. Needs to be completely covered."

Herbert would not be happy to be pulled away from what he was doing twice in one day, but it had to be done. Shane needed to show Ventura that he wasn't lying. Also, that iron was not an effective weapon. It was a lucky break that the man hadn't been murdered yet if he thought he was some kind of Ghostbuster by just wielding a chunk of metal.

"Ryan..." Ventura said, staring at the cameo.

"You can play this as an FBI agent or a man who sees the dead, but this case won't let you do both. Cover it in salt. We don't have all day."

The agent's jaw tightened but he nodded eventually and began tearing apart the small paper packets. He poured one on the cameo and then another and another until there was a small pile of salt visible on the desk.

"Do I need more salt?" Ventura asked when he emptied the last one.

Shane shook his head.

"No. Now brush off the salt."

Ventura scoffed, annoyed by the instructions.

"Just do it. This is it. Last thing you need to do."

"Of course it is. I brush the salt away, and a spirit appears," the agent joked, swiping the pile with the side of his hand.

The salt spilled across the desk and exposed the cameo. Herbert appeared immediately between the men. He was facing Shane and looked frustrated.

"Why did you do that again?" he demanded. Shane shrugged awkwardly.

"Wasn't me," he answered, nodding forward. Herbert turned. He was eye to eye with Ventura, and it was hard to tell who looked more stunned by the appearance of the other.

"Oh, my God," Ventura whispered.

"What do I do?" Herbert asked, cocking his head to one side to speak to Shane.

"If someone could get me out of these cuffs, that would be great."

"You're here," Ventura said, ignoring Shane. He raised a hand as though intending to touch the big man but stopped himself. "I thought you were dead."

"I am," Herbert replied, still unsure of what was happening.

"Oh. Ha. Ha, yes!" Ventura said, smiling. "I've never... I've talked to them some before. But it's not always easy."

"You're lucky; some of them talk your ear off," Shane pointed out.

After a moment's hesitation, Ventura reached out, his fingertips passing through Herbert's chest with no resistance. Though he could see spirits, he could not interact with them. It put him at a decided disadvantage, especially for someone intent on investigating murders committed by ghosts. Nothing would hold Lisette back from harming him, while he could not damage her at all.

"It's cold," Ventura said.

"Please stop doing that," Herbert asked him, backing up a step.

"Oh. I'm sorry," the other man said. "Does it... hurt?"

"No, it's just odd," Herbert explained. "What is happening here?"

"Trying to convince Agent Ventura here that I'm not a serial killer and Lisette is going to kill a lot more people if he doesn't let me go."

"How is you being free going to help, Ryan?"

Herbert frowned and turned to look at Shane.

"He doesn't know?"

"He doesn't know."

"Know what?" Ventura asked.

"Shane can destroy ghosts. He can stop her. That's what we've been trying to do since…"

"Nashua," Shane said.

"Earlier for me, I suppose. I just didn't know how," Herbert added.

"You can destroy them? How?" Ventura demanded.

"Just a skill I have," Shane explained. "I can help you here, Ventura. I really can."

"You've been linked to multiple homicides, Ryan."

"How? Has anyone seen me kill someone?"

"Witnesses placed you at the scene—"

"You've been at the same scenes. A third of them, I was there days or weeks later. The way a person following leads would be. We're arguing in front of a giant man who just appeared out of thin air. I don't know what else you need to prove that this isn't what you think."

"I can't let a suspect go because he can destroy ghosts. There's no line in the reports I need to file that covers that."

"Is there one that says to pull me in here and ask about the Cult of the Endless Night? You're walking a line, and I get it. Pick a side, though. Either take me in, leave this hospital, and know that someone else is going to die, or get the cuffs off of me."

"We have enough circumstantial evidence to put you away for the rest of your life," Ventura told him.

"You'll have a building full of corpses here by tomorrow morning."

"So you say. If this ghost is so hell-bent on murder, why now? Why not over all these years leading up to today?"

"She's free now," Herbert answered. "We had her contained before. Until Bart let her go."

"Who is Bart?"

"Hartwell. Did your courthouse witnesses mention a second man? That was him. He's in love with the ghost," Shane explained. "He set her free."

"She has a living accomplice? You never mentioned that."

"Does it make a difference now?"

"I don't want to rush whatever is happening here if it's going badly for us, but we don't have time. The children weren't listening to me," Herbert told Shane. "They're going after others."

"Whoa, what children?"

"Ghost kids haunting the hospital. They've already killed a nurse and parents up in cardiology," Shane explained.

"And radiology," Herbert added.

"Children?" Ventura said quietly.

"*Ghost* children," Shane clarified. "You have to let me go."

Ventura grimaced like he had a foul taste in his mouth and made a sound to match. He approached Shane and put a hand on his shoulder, pushing him to one side as he fished out his handcuff keys.

"I swear to God, if you're playing me—"

"You can come back and haunt me," Shane told him.

The keys clicked in the cuffs, and they came loose on one wrist. Ventura frowned.

"Haunt you? You'd kill me?"

"If I was a serial killer, yes. Of course. I'd be stupid not to."

Ventura unlocked the other wrist and stepped back as Shane pulled his hands around front, dropping the cuffs on the desk.

"If we're going to do this, I need to know what's going on. Top to bottom, give me the whole story."

"We don't have time," Herbert said, more to Shane than Ventura.

"Make time. I've got carnivals and ghost children and arson and a hell of a lot more. I'm going to need to spin away from you and from ghosts to a believable story or we're all screwed," Ventura said.

"Well, not me. Probably," Herbert pointed out. "I'll be fine."

"Just give him the rundown," Shane said.

"As you like, sir," the big ghost replied. "Keeping in mind we have no time."

He broke into an extremely brief synopsis of what had happened with Lisette and Dash in the town of Burkitt, the subsequent imprisonment of the ghost, and the chain of murders that followed her release, thanks to Bart Hartwell. The story was concise and devoid of much detail, and Ventura had to stop him several times for clarification.

He caught the agent up to the events in the basement when they fought Lisette and then came upstairs upon hearing the Code Silver. Ventura took it mostly in stride, though his face was too expressive for his own good, and he struggled with the knowledge of what they were facing, or at least with how much he was willing to believe.

"Tell me something," Ventura said. He took a seat and leaned forward with his elbows on his knees, looking down rather than at Shane. "These other cases I've found where your name pops up. The docks in Boston. A goddamn army base in Montana. Were you involved? And were ghosts?"

"Yes," Shane answered simply.

"Both?"

"Yep."

Ventura lifted his head, and his expression was not what Shane expected. He looked sad, almost. But relieved.

"I've been following these cases. Not just yours, but others. The ones where things got written off, where witnesses say they saw these impossible things. I grab whatever ones I can find. They started calling me Mulder down in records because I want the weird ones. I've investigated werewolves that turned out to be dogs, and a vampire that was someone's downstairs neighbor who made a copy of their key. Ghosts that turned out to be old pipes, a crooked landlord, or mental illness."

His voice shook, and he cleared his throat.

"Until today, no one has shown me anything that can prove the things I see are real."

"Hell of a thing, huh?" Shane said.

Ventura laughed. He looked at Shane like he was seeing the man for the first time.

"You're so… casual. It's like nothing to you."

"I've been dealing with this for a very long time."

"But how is it not… how does it not tear you apart inside? The implications. This is amazing. This is beyond all we have ever known. This is proof of life after death. Of the human soul. You've seen things that could shake the foundation of humankind."

Shane glanced at Herbert, and the big man looked uncomfortable.

"I mean, if you put it that way," Shane said.

"How do you deal with it?"

The weight of the question hung in the air. For Ventura, this was a life-changing, even a world-changing, truth that Shane had just confirmed for him. For Shane, it was a pain in the ass. A murderous ghost who had run him ragged for far too long that he wanted to eliminate and be done with so he could go home.

"One of the first ghosts I ever saw tried to murder me in my own house," Shane told him. "Others have killed people I cared for. A lot of them, in fact. I've met ghosts that would have killed every living thing in the world if they had the chance, and people who would have helped them. So, for me, the shine of the miraculous truth of life after death has dulled a bit."

Ventura said nothing as Shane slipped the cameo back into his pocket as the intercom crackled.

"Code Silver to Internal Medicine. Code Silver, Internal Medicine," the voice said.

"We need to get people out of here," Shane said. Ventura shook his head.

"Standard procedure is a lockdown. It's anti-terrorism stuff to prevent a suspect from fleeing in the crowd."

"It's throwing meat to a wolf," Shane corrected. "Lisette wants victims. You lock this place down, it will be impossible to stop her, and she can just tear people apart one after another."

"If I start letting people out of here, my director is going to have my head."

"Keep them in, and you'll be trying to explain a mass murder committed by the dead."

Ventura gritted his teeth. His face had flushed red, and he looked like he might pass out.

"Goddamn it," he muttered. "Come on."

CHAPTER 18
MERCY OF THE DEAD

"I shouldn't be doing this," Ventura said.

He led Shane and Herbert away from the office and past the packed lobby full of people trying to get out. Police were standing guard at the entrance. Others approached Ventura to talk but were waved off. More than one gave Shane a look that suggested his face was now well-recognized.

"What choice do you have?" Herbert asked.

"Arrest you. Or Ryan, anyway. Take him to the police station, lock him up, and forget we ever met."

"You'd arrest a man you know is innocent?" Herbert asked.

Ventura scoffed, reading a board to see where he wanted to go.

"I don't know that. I know something else is going on, but that doesn't mean the two of you are innocent in all of this."

Shane had to laugh.

"Sounds like a cop," he said.

Ventura scowled and turned around, heading in the opposite direction and to the left.

"He's the only way you solve this case and stop people from dying," the big ghost explained.

"So you've said. And, as you can see, I took off the cuffs. Allow me a moment to wallow in my confusion and terror, please."

"I'm here because I want to end this," Herbert said.

There was pain in his voice, and Ventura stopped, fidgeted with his phone before turning to face the ghost.

"Those people in the carnival were my family. For over half a century, those were the people who cared for me. They laughed at my jokes and gave me a place to sleep and made me feel like I belonged somewhere. Before *and after* I died. I don't care if anyone ever knows my name, Agent Ventura. I just want to make sure no one else dies."

Ventura nodded, avoiding eye contact.

"I get it. I do. I want to help people, too, but the way I do that is as a federal agent, and that means I have to follow certain rules. I can't blame ghosts."

"No. But you can make up a story to fit the facts while serving justice. Isn't that more important than the rules?"

"Geez. This guy," Ventura said, forcing a laugh. Shane shrugged.

"He grows on you."

Ventura looked across the room, eyes darting from patients to police to Shane.

"Over here," he said at last, heading into a hallway away from the eyes of the others.

"You okay?" Shane asked.

Ventura seemed to get more worked up than he should have, but Shane was trying to keep in mind this was all very new for him.

"I told you I've been taking the weird cases, the ones that don't have answers or have unexplained phenomena as part of the entire story. This has been my life's work, okay? When I said no one has ever believed me, I meant it. I didn't believe myself for a long time. But I never experienced anything like this. Not in my wildest dreams did... I don't even know what to call this."

"Just a haunting. With some murders," Shane said. Ventura scoffed, shaking his head.

"'Just'? How do you even use that word? It's so normal for you. This ruined my life, Ryan. It has made me doubt my sanity since I was a kid. It made my parents treat me like I was broken, or mentally ill. I got made fun of for years. I still do at work. This was everything I ever needed to prove I'm not crazy!"

He was biting off his words now, teeth clenched and jaw tight, and Shane could feel the anger coming from him. He let the man finish and take some breaths.

"And now you have what you wanted, and you realize it can't make anything better in anyone else's eyes," Shane said.

"No. It can't."

"We're on the same boat, Ventura. Just different points in the voyage. My advice is to decide, right now, if you want to stay on. You can pretend you don't see anything. Sounds like it might be easy for you. You don't even know you see them half the time, you said so yourself. Choose to ignore it and live your life. Save people from the crimes of the living. It's still the same job. Or choose to deal with what you know and work with it. It's not easy, but you need to choose."

"I need so many drinks right now," the agent replied.

"I'll buy you one when we can walk out of here without someone freezing our faces off."

Behind Ventura, several paces down the hallway, a door opened slowly. The hinges produced a drawn-out squeal, and it caught the attention of the three men. Nothing happened for a long moment.

"What was that?" Ventura asked quietly.

In that hospital, if no one came through the door right away, then it was a safe bet it was nothing good.

"Help me," a voice whispered so quietly that it was almost inaudible.

Ventura took a step forward, and Shane grabbed his arm.

"Are you serious?" he asked.

"Someone's called for help," the agent replied.

Shane chuckled.

"If you're going to be dealing with ghosts, especially dangerous ones, you can't fall for something that obvious."

"Help me," the voice pleaded.

It sounded more strained this time, like someone in pain. The voice was female and there was something vaguely familiar about it, maybe a voice Shane had heard in passing.

"What if it's a patient or a family member or staff? Someone who was attacked?" Ventura countered. "We can't just not investigate."

"It's probably a ghost," Herbert suggested. "I think it's a ghost."

"This Lisette? The one killing everyone?"

"She doesn't talk much," Shane explained. "But the kids? Definite possibility."

"Oh, the short-haired girl," Herbert added.

Shane nodded and pointed at the big man.

"Buzz Cut. That's her voice. It's a ghost, and she wants to kill us."

"Can't imagine why," Ventura said, pulling his arm away.

"Please!" the girl cried.

Ventura snapped his head back and half ran to the open door.

"I understand that you're so used to this and jaded that you look at the world differently than I do, but I can't abandon someone who needs—"

Ventura didn't get to finish his sentence. Small, pale hands from the shadows gripped his ankles and pulled, and he fell backward as they dragged him into the room. He turned to face Shane, eyes wide in disbelief, but vanished through the doorway before he could utter a word. The door slammed shut after him.

Shane and Herbert shared only a glance. The ghost went through the wall into the room and Shane ran to the door. He slammed a booted foot against the wood, right below the handle, and it shuddered. With a grunt, he did it again and then again. Something snapped in the jamb, and one last kick broke the frame and forced the door open.

Ventura was pinned to the wall the way Shane had been stuck to the pipes in the sub-basement. Little hands had emerged from nowhere, holding him in place. One covered his mouth while another pulled at his throat. Others kept his wrists and ankles locked in place.

Buzz Cut stood in front of him, her back to Shane, with Herbert at her side.

"—because it's your choice," Herbert said. The girl looked at the big ghost and her expression was nothing short of rage.

"Exactly. My choice," she replied, before turning to look back at Shane.

"You're never getting out of here alive," she told him.

She reached for Ventura then, and Shane only made it a step toward her before Herbert's fist came down like a hammer on her head. The girl collapsed, and the ghosts holding Ventura loosened their grips enough for the man to slip loose. Only a couple of hands held, but when they realized the others had given up, they let him go.

"I'm sorry you died here," Herbert told the girl, "but that doesn't mean more people have to."

She lashed out at him from the floor, and he lifted a leg, stomping his foot on her arm at the elbow. The sound made Herbert and Ventura wince. Her forearm hung limply, and she screamed in anger.

"This isn't about you," she yelled at Herbert. The big man nodded.

"It is, though."

He kicked her in the jaw, causing her to roll back against the wall. Shane had been ready to attack, to defend Ventura and destroy the ghost if necessary, but Herbert had surprised him.

"You can go. But just this once. I can't let you leave if you do this again," Herbert told the girl.

Shane did not agree that letting her go was the best course of action, but this was Herbert's show, so he let the big ghost play it the way he wanted to. He just hoped the ghost was making the right call. The girl was angry, and there was every reason to believe she was going to stay that way.

Buzz Cut scowled and scuttled away, vanishing into the shadows.

Ventura cleared his throat roughly and rubbed his wrists where the hands had restrained him.

"Is this usual for you guys?" he asked.

"Not me," Herbert answered. "My life was relatively calm until recently."

"You?" Ventura said, looking at Shane.

"They usually try harder to kill me," he replied. "It's kind of nice to see it happen to someone else."

The agent touched the wall where he'd been pinned.

"Still cold," he said, more to himself than the others. He turned back to face Shane. "I don't know what I'm doing. I can't make a joke about it like you do."

"Not yet," Shane admitted. "You ever hear that saying about laughing so you don't scream?"

Ventura grunted.

"You don't have to do anything," Herbert suggested. "We will find Lisette and stop her. We just need you to give us space to do it."

Herbert understood Shane was useless if a hospital full of cops was constantly looming over his shoulder and everyone suspected him of being a murderer. Ventura had the power to sway how things played out.

"I have to do something," the agent said. "How could I go back to the way things were now? I can't forget what I know to be true."

"Then I think you know what to do," Shane told him. "And we can't keep wasting time. It's time to make a rash decision under pressure."

"This is insane," Ventura replied.

"Always," Shane agreed. "So, what now?"

Ventura let out a long, shuddering breath. His hands were shaking, and he looked like he might throw up until he took a few long, deep breaths and nodded.

"Okay. I'm doing this. We're doing this. We go to the admin and tell them we're letting the people leave. I'll have local PD in the parking lot checking everyone on the way out. I need a description of this Hartwell."

"Done," Shane said.

"Once the coast is clear, you're going to need to show me how to find a ghost that doesn't want to be found. I'm in this all the way or I can't help at all. Understood?"

Shane looked at Herbert, who nodded.

"Just keep in mind, she can kill you and you have no way to fight back if you get cornered."

"I won't get cornered, then," Ventura said.

He had put aside his doubts and was now calm and confident. The man did an excellent job of covering his fear with the patina of knowledge and preparedness.

"This is fun," Herbert said. "It's like we're a team."

"Not a team," Ventura corrected. Shane nodded his agreement.

"Yeah, no. But I appreciate the sentiment," he said. "Now let's get moving."

CHAPTER 19
LOCKDOWN

"This is not our operating procedure."

"I didn't ask you if it was," Ventura said.

The director of the hospital was a woman named Shelly Merchant. She wore a business suit, had her hair pulled as tight as anything Shane had ever seen, and her face had a permanent scowl. Not that he could blame her under the circumstances.

As far as anyone on staff knew, there had just been separate attacks in the building conducted by an assailant no one could describe. Five people were dead.

"These procedures were devised with the FBI, Agent Ventura. Your agency. Law enforcement is alerted, the building is locked down, and the investigation proceeds."

"This case is atypical, Ms. Merchant. Our suspect is still at large and still committing attacks despite police presence. It would be better to ignore that protocol and evacuate," Ventura explained.

"This is a terrorism response, Agent. My hands are tied."

"You'll be lucky if your hands aren't cut off and tossed in a trash bag," Shane pointed out. The director looked at him as though he threatened to be the one to do it and Ventura winced again, turning to face him.

"You're not helping," he said.

"Sounded menacing," Herbert added.

"Kind of need to be menacing before someone else gets gutted."

"Who are you?" Merchant demanded.

"Someone who doesn't want to see everyone who works here

murdered. Figured you'd be on board," Shane answered.

"I'm sorry, are you with the FBI as well, Mister…?"

"Ryan. No. But listen, what was the name of that nurse in the basement?" he asked. Merchant was confused by the question, though Shane was not even asking her. Herbert rubbed the back of his head a moment.

"I think her ID said Keeley?"

"Nurse Keeley?" Shane said.

"What about Nurse Keeley?" the director asked.

"Looks like she killed a good deal of your patients over the years. Pillow smotherings, wrong medications, things like that."

Merchant's eyes flashed anger, and she glared at a man in a suit standing with her, who no one had introduced. Shane was willing to put money on him being the hospital's lawyer.

"You cannot make accusations—" the man in the suit began and Shane pointed at him.

"Oh, there it is. You are a lawyer, and you're going to ramble on about defamatory statements or something. Except your boss gave you that, 'Who's he been talking to?' look that tells me this has come up before. Maybe someone was suspicious about how many of Nurse Keeley's patients kept turning up dead, you looked into it and couldn't find much, so you sent her to a different department or something?"

"Mr. Ryan—" Merchant said icily.

"Have you had suspicions that an employee of this hospital has been harming patients?" Ventura interrupted.

"Of course not," the lawyer answered for her. "Internal matters are dealt with through established systems—"

"She's dead," Shane said, not wanting a long-winded answer to throw them off-track. The lawyer shut his mouth instantly, and even Ventura looked surprised by the revelation.

"Someone gutted her in the sub-basement. Old boiler room. That's what you're dealing with right now. That's what's going to happen to everyone here, staff included. What with blocked doors and all these anti-terrorism protocols. So let the people evacuate. Don't make it easy for the killers."

Ventura got a call on his phone just as Shane finished, lifting it to his ear.

Merchant and the lawyer lowered their voices and talked among themselves while Herbert whispered as well, though it was unnecessary.

"Won't this work better if we don't panic everyone?"

"They're already panicking. They need to know everyone is at risk."

"We have all the exits free now," Ventura said, hanging up the phone. "Local police are covering each exit and are going to coordinate the evacuation."

"Agent Ventura—" Merchant began, anger overtaking fear in her voice.

"I'm running this operation, Ms. Merchant, with or without your help. Your lawyer can note your dissent, but things will be a lot easier with your help."

Merchant sighed loudly and covered her face with her hands.

"I'm here to help, Agent Ventura. I want to make sure everyone is okay. My job is helping people. You understand that, right?"

"Mine too," he told her. "Can we get an announcement over the intercom telling people to leave through the front exit in an orderly fashion?"

"Sure," she said.

He left her to get to her work and took Shane and Herbert back down the hall to the lobby.

"I need to touch base with my team. We'll try to filter everyone out these doors. I'll have teams on exits other than the front, and we'll stop anyone who tries to leave, but I need you to just be patient for five minutes and not say anything horrifying to anyone. Please," Ventura said.

"Got it," Shane replied. "Maybe cancel that APB on me while you're at it."

Merchant's announcement came over the hospital intercom, alerting everyone except for essential staff and patients unable to leave to evacuate immediately. The crowd in the lobby became so loud that most of the message couldn't be heard, but anyone elsewhere in the hospital would have known what to do.

Shane watched Ventura pull in the police officers and dole out commands. He was remarkably decisive when dealing with living problems. He was probably good at his job, Shane thought. As long as it didn't throw him too many curveballs.

There was an eagerness to Ventura, and it read to Shane as an excitement that the man didn't want to acknowledge. He had been holding the other part of his life inside for years, and Shane understood that fear. And that was why he also recognized there was more to it than Ventura was willing to admit.

Part of Ventura had hoped he was crazy, that he'd been seeing things that weren't real his whole life. At least then he'd have an explanation, even if it was a bad one. But learning the truth had spun him around a little.

There was horror, of course. Fear of the terrifying unknown. But there was also relief and excitement. The only thing better than thinking you're crazy is knowing you're not.

Ventura wanted to explore that world; Shane could feel it. He could pretend otherwise or try to control those emotions and be more reasonable and more responsible. But no one knew better what it was like to be immersed in the world of the dead than Shane Ryan.

Shane was by no means in the market for some kind of apprentice, especially not an FBI agent. He'd worked with enough people who could see the dead, even those who couldn't, to know what a dangerous road that was to walk. He didn't need to watch someone else die.

Because of that, he didn't want Ventura to walk into that world blind.

He had to prepare him at least a little, if for no other reason than to pay him back for getting him off the hook for Lisette's murders. Assuming Ventura could do that.

If Ventura wanted to be a part of that world, if he didn't want to turn his head and ignore the spirits he saw when he saw them, then he'd need to be a little more prepared. Lucky for him, he was in for a hands-on crash course.

The police dispersed to cover the exits, and those at the front started allowing people to leave. Herbert gave Ventura a remarkably precise description of Bart Hartwell, and Ventura had the officers be on the lookout for anyone who met it.

Shane knew there was no chance Hartwell was leaving the hospital, certainly not through the front door, but he was happy to let Ventura take control of the evacuation.

Angry and scared patients and visitors filed out as quickly as they could, and staff came shortly after. There was little turmoil during the evacuation, only a few shoving matches that were quelled quickly.

By the time Merchant was ready to leave, the lobby had been all but emptied.

"We're going to be set up in the parking lot by that light over there," Merchant told Ventura at the door. "I've got our legal department, public relations, and facilities manager at the ready if you need anything. We need to coordinate care for patients who could stay at home and redirect others. There are still more than a dozen critical patients we cannot move that you need to be aware of."

"You can't transfer them to another hospital?" Ventura asked.

"Critical patients," Merchant said again. "These children are hanging on by a thread. Two are in surgery, and one is on life support after a serious accident this afternoon. Teams are staying with them, doctors and nurses who understand the risk and why the hospital is being evacuated, but they will not leave their patients to die."

There was a hint of challenge in her voice like she wanted Ventura to try and force her to fully evacuate. Instead, the FBI agent nodded.

"I'll need room numbers, so I know where to send officers to keep an eye on them."

She handed him a slip of paper with the information already prepared.

"Find the person doing this, Agent Ventura. I want my hospital back."

She looked at Shane then, disdain on her face, but said nothing more. Instead, she and the lawyer left. Only Shane and Ventura remained in the lobby. Two police officers stayed at the door, and Herbert waited off to one side.

"You ready for this?" Shane asked as the automatic doors closed.

"God, no. I don't even know what we're doing," Ventura said. He took out his phone and quickly called someone, relaying information about the still-occupied rooms.

"Yeah, me either," Shane said, turning to look at the empty lobby. He had no clue where to start. He didn't think Hartwell and Lisette were in the sub-basement.

It seemed that Hartwell had been with Lisette long enough to know how she worked and the best ways to keep her hidden. They would have chosen something unpredictable. The sub-basement was too obvious, especially with the kids down there. That had been a red herring.

"Are these people safe outside?" Ventura asked. He was still looking out the doors. Many people had backed away, across the parking lot. The staff was congregating, and many patients and families looked to be waiting for the all-clear so they could return.

"No," Shane answered.

"Why not?"

"Unless they back off a good mile, it doesn't matter that we evacuated. That was just to make it easier for us to search."

"A mile?"

"Lisette is probably tied to Hartwell right now. He's carrying her around with him like I am Herbert. She'll be able to stray about a mile but no more."

"I can't get these people a mile away, Ryan. I don't even—"

"I know," Shane interrupted. "Not suggesting we do that. Lisette is less likely to go after them out there. Especially when there are people still in here. Kids in trouble, kids who are hurt, that's what's motivating her. If these ones are in such bad shape that they can't be moved, that's where she's going, and kill whoever she thinks is responsible for their suffering."

"Then let's go stop her," Ventura said, holding up the list of rooms that were still in use.

He started toward the nearest elevator when Herbert grabbed his arm. Ventura gasped, the cold settling into his flesh, and Herbert held fast.

"You seem like a good man, Mr. Ventura. I don't want you to be afraid to run away."

"What's that supposed to mean?" he asked.

"If you see the black shadow, you need to run. It won't be like the children. She won't try to scare you, or threaten you, or anything. She'll just kill you. It will happen fast if you let it."

He let go of the man's arm and Ventura pulled it close to his body, cradling it and rubbing his other hand across it to warm up.

"Is that true?" he asked Shane.

"Oh yeah. She'll kill you dead."

CHAPTER 20
A TASTE FOR DEATH

Shane pressed the button for the elevator, and the three of them waited in the hallway, a sense of tension beginning to build. Ventura was trying to keep up his relaxed persona, but it wasn't working too well.

The lights flickered at the end of the hall, and Shane could feel the air growing colder. One of the overhead bulbs buzzed and snapped and then went dark. The next light flickered, slightly closer to the elevator bay and only a handful of lights away.

"Is that her?" Ventura asked. Shane shook his head.

"Bit too theatrical for her. Children, I think," Shane replied. The ghosts of children could be just as brutal as the adults, but they also had a habit of bigger set-ups and putting more effort into terrorizing a victim before ending things. Shane blamed horror movies and pop culture.

The elevator opened, and Herbert got in right away. Shane looked at the small space and then at the flickering light in the hall.

"What's wrong?" Ventura asked, joining Herbert. Shane shook his head and got in. Ventura's crash course was about to begin whether he liked it or not.

The doors closed, and Ventura pressed the button for their floor. The car ascended and Shane waited.

The music playing over the speakers got louder, an instrumental version of some pop hit from at least a decade earlier, slowed down slightly, and made friendlier with flutes and violins. The volume continued to rise until it became uncomfortable.

"Can we turn this off?" Ventura yelled, covering his ears. Shane looked at the speaker in the ceiling. If he had something to destroy it with, he would have. He didn't suspect Ventura would be keen on shooting his gun in an elevator, either.

The car rattled, and the two living occupants stumbled. Shane grabbed the safety rail on the wall and looked up at the digital display above the door. The numbers went up floor by floor, the speed of their ascent substantially increased.

His stomach felt like it was being pulled down at a faster rate than the rest of his body as the numbers of the display continued to climb. The fifth floor became the sixth, seventh, and eighth. Ventura held a rail and pointed at the display.

"That's not possible," he yelled over the music. They were passing the thirteenth floor, and the numbers continued to tick by. The hospital did not have that many floors.

The music became distorted, the instruments producing screeching, jarring sounds as the display raced through levels that didn't exist. The pressure on Shane's stomach increased, and he felt like gravity was trying to crush him.

Ventura was close to hyperventilating. Shane knew that telling him to calm down would help little. Fear was not so easily controlled. He needed to face it head-on. It would happen soon enough.

The elevator stopped. Shane could not say for sure if it had ever been moving or if the sensation was orchestrated by the spirits. The jolt was sudden and caused him to slam forcefully against the floor.

The overhead light failed, plunging the car into darkness.

"Eyes open, Herbert," Shane said from where he had collapsed in a corner.

"Of course," the ghost replied. "Nothing yet."

"You can see in here?" Ventura asked.

"I see everything."

"Good. Tell me when someone's about to kill me, please," Ventura requested.

"I will, sir," the ghost replied.

Shane got back to his feet and took a breath. The car was chilly, but Herbert was right next to him, and there was no way to avoid the cold. No way to tell if it was him or other spirits encroaching on the space.

Shane reached into his pocket and retrieved a cigarette from his pack. He slipped it between his lips and then lit it. Ventura's expression in the flickering light from the Zippo was about what he expected.

"Are you serious?" he asked.

"Been a while since I had a chance. Seemed like a good time," Shane answered.

He put away the lighter. The car returned to blackness, save for the orange glow of the tip of the cigarette as he smoked.

Ventura coughed in the darkness and Shane frowned. Herbert had never complained about his smoking because he didn't breathe. Shane didn't plan to stop, but he hoped Ventura figured out a way to handle it.

"Shane." Herbert's voice was tense.

"Stay in the middle, Ventura," Shane said, moving as close to Herbert as he could. The big ghost took up half of the elevator and though Shane could maneuver around him, Ventura was another matter.

"Why?"

"Natural camouflage," Shane answered.

A light sprang to life and Ventura held up his phone flashlight. The other ghosts were not visible, but something had spooked Herbert and Shane didn't need another warning.

"Middle," he said again.

"Herbert's in the middle," Ventura protested.

"That's my point."

Herbert and Ventura looked unsettled by the proposal, but Shane ignored them.

"I can't fight multiple opponents in this space and worry about them ripping off your face. Just get inside him."

Ventura looked at Herbert. The big ghost frowned and looked away.

"Just do it," he said. "Should have asked me first, though, Shane."

"There's no way," Ventura protested.

The music went dead. A low shushing sound replaced it, and the three men in the elevator stood, frozen, listening. It took Shane a moment to realize it was the sound of breathing. Strained, almost wet, but breathing nonetheless. Like the breathing of someone who was very sick.

Ventura turned his light to look around the elevator car, but there was nothing to see, not even the walls. Darkness surrounded them on every side. The beam of light illuminated only a short distance and nothing more than the tiled floor. The walls were gone. They were in a vast emptiness.

As in the basement, when Ventura moved the light, there were the faintest signs of movement. Things darting from view too quickly to focus on or too far from the light to see clearly.

The eyes appeared then, golden and bright, and they blinked in and out of existence.

Shane took Ventura by the shoulder and forced him toward Herbert. Shane's hands could not pass through the ghost's body, but for Ventura, it was like nothing existed in that space. He was consumed by the big man's frame and gasped as the cold overwhelmed him.

"This doesn't seem like a good idea," Herbert pointed out.

"It'll do for now. Can you think of a safer place?"

"Anywhere else in the world. But for now… no."

A shape slipped from the darkness at the edge of Ventura's light and crept toward Shane, low to the ground. He had not seen the ghost when they were in the basement and it was older than the others, from the earliest days of the hospital based on the antiquated robe.

It did not look like a child. The ghost's body was ropey and muscular and bore the look of a hard life of labor. The body was thin, and through the back of the robe, Shane could see its ribs, running along a grossly protruding spine that gave it the look of a lizard with armored protrusions along its back.

The ghost moved on all fours, and its path was irregular. It would stop and start and then scuttle left or right. It had no hair on its head but bore deep scars across its scalp from some kind of brain surgery it must have endured. Shane couldn't tell if it was male or female.

"Whatever Lisette told you, you don't have to listen to her," Herbert told the ghost. It cocked its head to one side, neither of its eyes focusing on the big man. They were skewed and unfocused, one pupil severely dilated and the other surrounded by a spiderweb of thin, red veins.

The ghost opened its mouth and produced a series of guttural clicks and moans. If it was trying to produce words, it simply could not approximate anything even close to English.

Shane flexed his fingers, running the edge of his thumb along the smooth iron of his ring. He kept his eyes locked on the ghost, and it continued to jerk and scuttle this way and that as it crept closer to them.

When it was just a few feet away, Shane moved to close the gap, not content to let the ghost control when and how it would attack. He put himself between the ghost and Herbert, his hand clenched into a fist as he prepared for a fight.

The ghost wailed like a wild animal warning the rest of its pack. Half howl and half scream, it was long and resonant and made Shane wince as the pitch continued to rise.

The ghost rose with it, standing upright and exposing its chest and stomach. The robe the spirit wore was saturated with blood on the front and torn from collar to knee. Something had torn the ghost's body to shreds, and its innards bulged at the edges of the deep wounds.

Ventura swore and dropped his light. The ghost lunged the moment darkness gave it cover, arms wide as though trying to embrace Shane.

The attack caught Shane off-guard. He swung his fist but missed his mark as the ghostly body crashed into him, hitting him well before his fist had a chance to make contact.

The spirit clicked and groaned, its face touching his. Cold, clammy hands latched onto Shane's wrists and pinned him to the floor as its bony knees dug into his leg muscles and kept him immobile.

He head-butted the ghost, forcing it to grunt in surprise though the hit did little damage. For its size, the ghost was stronger than he had expected.

Shane felt something like probing fingers against his chest. More and more of them poked and prodded at his chest and sides and stomach, each one cold and firm and applying more and more pressure.

Still huddled within Herbert's body, Ventura got control of his light once again and shone it on Shane and his attacker.

"Oh, good God," he muttered.

In the light, Shane could see what Ventura saw. The ghost's organs protruded from the wounds in its torso. The viscera moved like fingers and arms and gripping appendages, pulling and poking at Shane.

The attack seemed weak at first, designed more to look uncomfortable than to feel that way, but the more Shane struggled, the more he realized that the pressure was only increasing. Each cold, moist, spongy bit of the ghost's insides pushed against Shane and then continued to push.

He could feel the pressure building along his side as lengths of intestine tried to force their way between and under his ribs. It was like a gentle nudge at first, but then it grew unpleasant and finally painful.

Shane felt his flesh stretching and his ribs being forced up. If the assault continued, the intestines would break the skin and puncture his body, fracturing ribs in the process.

Ventura emerged from inside of Herbert's frame. Shane's teeth were gritted as he attempted to do anything, even bite the monstrosity on top of him, with no success in getting the upper hand.

Shane watched as the FBI agent pulled an iron bar from his pocket and brought it down hard on the ghost's head. The ghost was forced out of space like darkness being banished by a light. It simply ceased to exist, and Shane was left on the floor, gasping in the wake of the relieved pressure.

There was no time to relax in the spirit's absence. It was not the only ghost who had come for them.

CHAPTER 21
CRASH COURSE

"There's still no door," Herbert said.

The ghosts had co-opted the elevator, making it part of an illusion of emptiness, which made it a prison. There was nowhere to escape to in the vast space in what was ironically a very small space in real life.

"This can't be happening," Ventura said after offering Shane a hand to get to his feet.

The agent made his way toward the walls, or tried to, but found nothing. He walked a short distance with his arms extended, as far as he dared from his companions, expecting to find an invisible wall.

"Doesn't need to make sense," Shane explained, checking his sides for wounds. The ghost had not broken skin, but there were pinpoint bruises that felt like he'd been hit with hammers.

"It has to make sense. This is an elevator, and it's small. There are walls here, and a door. Ghosts can't just change physics."

Shane had to laugh.

"No? Care to explain why?"

"Because it doesn't make sense," Ventura said again.

"Herbert died in the seventies, was it?" Shane asked. The big ghost nodded. "The seventies. You were just inside of a ghost that died in the seventies who's still walking around and talking and all that good stuff. No one can see him but you and me. You're going to lose your mind if you try to root any of this in what you think you know about science and logic."

Ventura turned, dropping his arm that searched for the door that should have been there but was not.

"All of a sudden, everything we believe is a lie, and only you and me and whoever else can see the world for what it is know the truth?"

"God, no," Shane replied. "I don't know anything about how spaceships work. Or curing cancer. Or building a computer. Science is still science, Ventura. The world still has rules. What we have here is a case of how the rules haven't been understood or explained yet. We're like cavemen discovering fire. You might not understand why it happens, but you sure as hell better respect that it can kill you."

A child's laughter erupted and Ventura rejoined the other two quickly, turning his back to them so he could use the light of his phone to look into the darkness and see what was coming for them.

"But you can interact with them. You can touch them, fight them. You said you can destroy them. Why can't I?"

"Like I said, rules that haven't been written. I didn't practice this or try to cultivate it, but it's the only reason I'm still alive. I learned that it works, and I use it to protect myself when I can."

"You ever think the fact you can do this stuff is the reason your life is always in danger?"

Shane grunted. Of course he'd thought that, but he knew it wasn't true. When he was a child and a ghost tried to kill him, he had not been some wandering existential threat to the dead. He was just someone a malevolent thing wanted to destroy. Just like so many others. Few wanted to kill him because he was Shane Ryan. Not at first, at least. They wanted to kill him because he was alive. They wanted to kill everyone because they were alive.

"Wish it was that simple," Shane answered.

"Isn't it? There has to be a reason ghosts want to hurt people, and why these ones want to kill us."

"Why?" Shane asked.

The question stumped Ventura for a moment and the ghosts used the silence as an opportunity to laugh again. Closer now, and more of them.

They were trying to create fear and unease.

"What do you mean why?" Ventura asked.

"Why does a ghost need a reason to hurt someone?"

Ventura scoffed.

"Every killer has a motive. Doesn't need to be a good one, but they all have one."

"Some ghosts like to kill, Ventura. That's a good thing to keep in mind. A ghost and a person who was once alive are not the same thing. Some ghosts are like Herbert. The person dies, and they come back, and it's like nothing changed. But some can't make that transition the right way. Some leave the human part of themselves in the ground, and when they come back, they are something new. Darker. Angrier."

"But why? Why is Herbert a good guy and Lisette a monster?"

"Why are you a good guy and the guy who murders his family a monster? Even science isn't going to tell you why some people are horrible and some aren't. There's too much happening that we can never know."

"Great," Ventura said, sarcasm clear. "I have to spend the rest of my life wondering if every ghost I see is going to want to tear out my heart."

"Yes, you are," Shane agreed.

A ghost's glowing eyes appeared in the periphery of Ventura's light. A second set appeared behind the first.

"If they can make this illusion, then how do we escape? How do we win this scenario?" Ventura asked. He still hadn't quite grasped the situation. Shane wasn't sure anyone could, right off the bat. How do you explain the inexplicable?

The answer was as simple for Shane as it was impossible for someone like Ventura. He'd just have to watch and see.

"Let's just get this over with," Shane said.

The ghosts obliged. The children were predictable enough in their attacks. Hands reached from the dark as they had before. Shane crouched low and punched the back of one small, pale hand. The iron ring forced it back to where it came from.

He backhanded a second set of clutching fingers, banishing a second spirit before using his other hand to grab the wrist of a third and pull it from the shadows. The spirit he pulled free looked to be a young man of maybe sixteen or seventeen. His face was as white as a fish's belly and long, brown hair was plastered to it as though he'd just come from a swim.

"We won't let you hurt her," the boy said, brown water gurgling from his mouth as he spoke.

"Protecting her now instead of her protecting you? That doesn't sound very motherly," Shane replied. He twisted the ghost's arm around and pinned him to the ground, kneeling on the spirit's back between his shoulders to keep him in place.

"Is that the plan now?" Shane asked, scanning the darkness. "You risk yourselves for this ghost you don't even know?"

"She's going to free us," the pinned ghost said. Shane looked down at him.

"What the hell does that mean?"

"She'll take us away. She promised to get us out of this hospital. We can be outside again. We can go anywhere we want."

"And you believed that?" Shane asked. The ghost growled, but it came out wet and bubbly as more water spilled from his mouth.

"She came from the outside. She didn't die here. She can go anywhere, and she'll take us."

"To her carnival?" Herbert asked. The ghost had limited mobility and couldn't see Herbert.

"Yes! She said she owns a carnival. We can all travel the country together and be like a family. Not be stuck here to watch more kids die over and over and over."

Herbert sighed as more ghosts moved at the edges of the light.

"She burned it, you know. The carnival is gone. She killed everyone in it."

"Good," the ghost spat. "Then nobody will bother us."

"Going to drive a truck, are you?" Shane asked. "That'd be fun to watch."

"She has help. The man who brought her here will help us, too. She promised."

"Who, Bart Hartwell? The old, broken man who carries her around?" Shane asked. "He's never getting out of here alive. You have to know that."

"She promised," the ghost insisted.

"The hospital is surrounded by the police," Ventura said. "We have his description. He can't get out of here. What she promised you is impossible."

One of the other ghosts came forward. It was the boy Shane had met in the morgue. He looked angry but also afraid.

"I told you she was a liar," the boy yelled. He was not speaking to Shane and the others; he was speaking to the drowned ghost. "I told you she threatened me."

"She's not a liar," the ghost yelled back. "Why would she lie?"

"Because all she wants to do is kill. And she can kill more by using you as weapons," Herbert answered.

"I don't want to do this anymore," the ghost from the morgue said. He didn't wait for a reply. Instead, he ran to the shadows and was gone. Shane watched others do the same, pulling away into the darkness.

The overhead light flickered above them, and the elevator walls morphed into existence. The drowned ghost bellowed, vomiting water across the floor, and thrashed in a rage.

"We have to kill them all," he roared, trying desperately to get Shane off his back. "Get back here, you cowards!"

Shane pushed the ghost's head firmly onto the ground and leaned forward, digging his knee between the spirit's shoulder blades.

"All she wants from you is death," Shane told him. The ghost laughed, spewing murky water across the floor.

"That's what she'll get," the ghost said.

He kicked his legs and tried to writhe free. There would be no talking him down. He believed Lisette's lie and would not see things as they were. It was probably easier for him to imagine that he was finally going to get a happy ending out of everything.

Shane grabbed the ghost's head firmly. He didn't look up to see if Ventura was watching, but he knew the man was. The agent needed to see how things played out, and what Shane brought to the table, needed to know why he could end things in a way no one else could.

The ghost's neck snapped as Shane jerked its head harshly to one side. He heard Ventura take in a breath but before the man could speak, Shane slammed his hands down. The ghost's skull crunched under the pressure, splitting like old fruit before the entire body burst.

The force of the spirit's destruction knocked Shane back against the wall of the elevator. Herbert and Ventura felt it as well. The unexpected release of power surprised them both and Ventura landed harshly, face-up on the floor.

"What the hell was that?" he asked, shakily trying to sit up. Shane took a moment to clear his head and then used the railing on the elevator wall to get back to his feet.

"A ghost can be destroyed. It releases a lot of energy, as you just saw, but it can be done."

Herbert had seen Shane destroy a spirit before today, but the big man still looked unsettled. Ventura, on the other hand, looked absolutely horrified.

"He exploded," the man said. "You blew him up."

"He blew up on his own," Shane corrected. "I didn't add anything to the mix."

"And it's permanent? It's not like with the iron?"

"Permanent," Shane said. "He won't be back."

The elevator dinged, and the pleasant, electronic voice told them they had reached their floor. The doors opened and Ventura stared out into one of the hospital's many pristine, empty hallways. It was as though nothing had happened.

The other ghosts had vanished. Whether they fled like the boy from the morgue or had been scared off by whatever happened to the drowned ghost, none chose to stay and fight.

"They might come back," Herbert pointed out, waiting for Ventura to exit the elevator. The agent needed a moment, but he finally stepped off the elevator, allowing Shane and Herbert to get off as well.

"Where do they go when they die like that?" Ventura asked, looking back into the elevator as the doors closed. It looked the same as it had when they first got on.

"I don't think they go anywhere," Shane answered. "I think that's the end. For real this time."

CHAPTER 22

OLD FRIENDS

The room number Merchant had given them was close, but the sound of running footsteps was closer. They were walking down a brightly lit hallway with windows overlooking the rear of the hospital. Outside, the flashing lights of a half-dozen police cars showed the edges of the barrier that local cops had created to keep people out of the hospital and prevent anyone else from leaving unexpectedly. They were on the eighth floor.

A middle-aged man in scrubs rounded a corner in a full panic, skidding to a stop so suddenly that he lost his footing and fell when he saw Shane and Ventura.

"Help me," the man pleaded, struggling to his feet and stumbling toward them. Ventura reached out and took hold of the man before he fell again, steadying him as he regained his footing.

"Sir, I'm Agent Ventura with the FBI. I need you to tell me what happened."

"Oh, thank God, the FBI," the man said, unable to catch his breath. "I was in Operating Room 6. I had an entire surgical team. We were performing an appendectomy on a patient who had gone septic, and this man came in. He had the patient's family held hostage, he took the surgical team at gunpoint, and then Nurse Geffen's face just burned. There was nothing there, and then a black handprint just burned into her face."

He ran through the narrative with a speed that made his words nearly unintelligible as he gasped for air the entire time.

"I ran. Nurse Geffen got lifted from the ground, and I just ran," he sobbed, looking into Ventura's face for some kind of explanation or absolution.

"Room six?" Ventura clarified. The doctor nodded and Ventura moved the man to one side. "Head downstairs to the front entrance. Tell the men at the door who you are and that I'm handling it. Go now."

He didn't wait for the doctor to respond. Instead, he pulled his gun from its holster and started forward, cautiously following the path they'd seen the doctor travel to reach them.

"How many people in a surgical team?" Ventura asked as he led Shane and Herbert down the hallway.

"Should have asked the doctor," Shane said. It didn't matter. He knew Hartwell, and he knew Lisette. Anyone else would be staff or the patient's family. It made it easier to determine who he needed to fight.

"You two get Hartwell under control," Shane said. "Don't let him shoot me."

"And you?" Ventura asked.

"I'll make sure Lisette doesn't burn off anyone else's face."

Someone screamed in the near distance, and Shane regretted the words he'd spoken. She wasn't waiting for him or anyone else to arrive.

Ventura ran, and Shane went with him. They had no time to be strategic, not if Lisette was killing everyone she could.

They reached Operating Room 6 and Shane nodded to Herbert, who moved through the wall as Ventura pushed open the doors with his gun sweeping the room.

"Don't make me kill you."

The words were out of Ventura's mouth before Shane even got an adequate look at the room's layout. He had to give the agent credit for having his cool movie lines down and lacking fear in the face of danger.

Shane stood next to him for only a moment, taking in as much of the scene as he could.

Two bodies were on the floor, both with black, frozen handprints burned into their faces. Ventura was steady as a rock, his gun aimed at Bart

Hartwell, who stood on the far side of the room holding his own weapon. His free arm was wrapped around a woman whose face was a mask of fear, tears streaming down her red cheeks as she gasped and cried. Hartwell's gun was pressed into the side of her head.

On the floor on the other side of the room were three more members of the surgical team and a man in street clothes. The man and Hartwell's hostage must have been the family of the patient, a boy, still unconscious and on the operating table while monitors beeped around them.

Lisette was at the boy's side, an irregular shadow in the middle of the room. Alongside Hartwell was another figure Shane recognized.

"Nils," Herbert said.

He had been planning a surprise attack from the opposite wall but revealed himself upon seeing his old friend. Nils had been at the carnival when Shane first arrived, one of the ghosts who loitered there. He had seemed friendly for a time, but they'd lost track of him after Hartwell and Lisette left with the carnival in tow.

"I will blow this woman's head off," Hartwell said, his voice shaky and full of anger. He squeezed his hostage more tightly and jammed the gun harder against her head. Ventura was unmoved.

"If you do that, you won't live to see her drop. There's one way to survive this, and you need to drop the gun to make it happen."

Lisette moved, the shadow flowing lithely, and Ventura cocked his weapon.

"If you think you can get out of here with your crony's brains still in his skull, then by all means, keep moving," he told the ghost.

Shane almost laughed. Ventura was ballsier than he had a right to be when faced with an opponent. He knew there was no way the agent was as confident as he was pretending to be, but he put on a hell of a show.

"Why are you here?" Herbert asked, ignoring what the others were doing and focusing on Nils. Shane was wondering the same, but he kept his attention focused on Lisette. Iron would do them no good if she attacked; it would only send her back to the same room, to wherever on his person Hartwell had stashed her comb. If they fought now, it would be for real.

Nils, a tall, skinny, and all-around nondescript man, had once been a ticket taker at the carnival. Someone had stabbed him to death during a robbery long ago, and his spirit remained. Much like Herbert, he had been a staple at Bartolomy and Sons for decades.

"What do you care, Herbert?" Nils replied.

Shane did not know the spirit well, but he had seemed level-headed and even kind before. Certainly friendly. Though the circumstance was not one conducive to happy reunions, there was something more at play. Nils looked and sounded angry, and his words were hateful as he spoke.

"I thought… we tried to save Artemis, but they killed him. Everyone was gone when we got back. I didn't know what happened to you," Herbert explained.

"What do you think happened?"

The woman in Hartwell's grip continued to sob, unaware of the spirits in the room with them, while Shane kept his eyes on Lisette. They didn't have time for a reunion, happy or unhappy. Something was going to tip the scales toward chaos at any moment.

"We left. It's not like I could run away, right?" Nils continued. While the living carnival workers might have had the choice at first—at least those who could escape before Lisette caught them—Nils was bound like any other ghost. There was nowhere he could run. Not really.

"But why are you here? You're helping them after what they did?"

Herbert sounded more than shocked. He sounded hurt. Nils shook his head, his expression sour and angry.

"What difference does it make? Are you telling me you don't have those thoughts sometimes? That urge to just kill? When you see or hear someone being a fool, or cruel, or just there when you don't want them there. Don't you ever want to reach out and just crush them?"

"No," Herbert said as though it was the most obvious thing in the world. "Of course not."

"Well, I do," Nils replied. "I feel it all the time, and I spent years forcing it down. Ignoring it. But who cares now? They're all gone. The carnival is gone, Herbert. Everyone is dead. Everyone."

"I know," the big man told him. "So why do you have to start killing people you don't even know? People who did nothing wrong?"

Lisette became agitated by Herbert's words. The shadowy body shuddered and swayed. It was hard to focus on. Shane took a step toward her, and Hartwell yelled, roughly jerking the hostage in his arms.

He spoke, but Lisette spoke over him, loud whispers that were still impossible to understand.

"They didn't do 'nothing'," Hartwell yelled. "They're not innocent."

"Of course they are," Herbert responded.

"No!" Hartwell yelled through gritted teeth. "Look at the boy."

Shane could see the child on the table. He was unconscious, and it looked like they had been able to at least finish the surgery. His wound, stitched up, was still exposed and not yet cleaned, but the procedure was done, and he was still breathing with a steady pulse.

"They saved him," Shane said. "He's alive."

Lisette's whispers grew louder and angrier. Hartwell sobbed and shook his head, almost growling between his clenched teeth.

"He almost died. They nearly let him die. Parents must protect children, not let them die."

"His appendix ruptured, how the hell was that his parents', or anyone else's fault?" Shane said incredulously. "This is how you take care of a kid with a medical emergency. You go to the hospital. Anything else would have killed him."

Shane turned from Hartwell to Lisette.

"You could have killed him by meddling mid-operation."

The ghost raged and Shane scoffed, turning back to Hartwell.

"What do you think happens to the kids of the people you two murdered already? They have no families now, so what does that mean? No one to put a roof over their heads. No one to feed them, clothe them, or take care of them. How many kids live in misery now because of you two? How many are going to die because of you two?"

Shane grabbed hold of the end of the boy's bed and pulled it away from Lisette.

"Move," he said to the hospital staff and the boy's father as he pulled it closer. Lisette hissed but Shane kept the bed between them. The staff used the bed as a shield and fell behind Shane and Ventura, near the door. The father wouldn't leave, however, and Shane moved to the side of the bed, pulling harder and undoing the leads to the monitors attached to the child's body.

Shane forced the bed through the doors, pushing it back until the head of the bed was at his side and the foot was in the hallway.

"Take him somewhere," Shane told the staff members and the father. The man's eyes were on his wife.

"I'll worry about her; you worry about your kid," Shane told him. The woman in Hartwell's arms let out a faint cry.

"Go," she told her husband. The man followed Shane's instruction.

Ventura's aim had not wavered. His gun on Hartwell was the only thing keeping everything as calm as it was. No one wanted to risk making the first move.

Lisette drifted closer to Nils and Hartwell. The whispering continued. Hartwell's face was beet red and sweat glistened on his brow. His hands shook, but he held the woman fast and didn't drop the weapon an inch.

"You can't save them," Nils said. There was hopelessness in the ghost's voice that had not been there when Shane first met him. "I can follow them. I can kill them all before you could even blink."

"Jesus, Nils. Why?" Herbert asked.

"Because we're dead, Herbert," Nils shot back. "We pretended for decades that we weren't, but we are. Why do you care who lives or who doesn't? You're dead. You've been dead for a long time, and it means nothing. It. Means. Nothing."

"It means everything," Herbert countered.

Nils made a disgusted sound and turned his back on his former friend.

"It means nothing," he said to Shane. "And when I kill that boy, you'll see that I'm right."

CHAPTER 23
LIFE AND DEATH

Lisette's whispers rose to a furious pitch, and for the first time, Shane could understand what she was saying. The word "no" came scratchy and layered, over and over on itself like she spoke with many voices. But it was clear she was enraged.

The shadow moved toward Nils and Ventura took a step forward, his arm rock-steady as he aimed point-blank between Hartwell's eyes. He shook his head, his expression blank.

"I've shot people for less," Ventura said. His tone did not brook any argument. Shane believed what he said, and it seemed to have the desired effect on even the dead. Lisette stopped, while Nils crept behind Hartwell.

"You stay put, Nils," Hartwell ordered. "You stick to the plan."

"The plan," Nils scoffed. "What are you even talking about, old man?"

"You listen to her! You listen to Lisette, and this will all turn out fine, hear me? She knows what she's doing."

Hartwell's voice cracked, and there was no conviction in it. He might as well have been trying to convince himself rather than the ghost.

"Stop playing, old man. Why are we doing this? Lisette?" Nils asked, looking at the shadow. "Why keep up the act?"

"There's no act," Hartwell assured him.

Hartwell could no longer see Nils and it was making him nervous, but he refused to take his eyes off Ventura and his gun. Nils crept along the wall behind him, and Hartwell was visibly more uneasy as a result.

"It doesn't matter who dies. Everyone dies; who knows that better than us? What are we protecting children for? For Dash? Shane wasn't wrong. You're not saving them. Kill a child's parents and you might as well kill the child with them."

"No," Hartwell barked, accented by the whispers of Lisette behind him. "That ain't what this is for."

"Come off it," Nils said with a humorless laugh. "What is it for, then? This isn't about Dash's memory. Uncaring parents didn't kill those boys in Burkitt. It wasn't what made those people turn on your boy, Lisette. I saw what did it. Herbert saw it. Tell them."

Nils held out a hand to Herbert, but the big ghost could only shake his head.

Lisette's shadows swirled about her vague form like a storm confined to a single space.

"WHAT. DOES. THAT. MEAN?"

Her words sounded like they came from inside Shane's head rather than the outside world. It was the clearest she had been since he'd met her, and the anger was just as fierce as ever.

"It was a ghost, for God's sake," Nils continued. "Did no one ever tell you? It was a thing, some… twisted, horrible thing from Burkitt. That's what killed those boys. That's what whispered poison into the ears of the townspeople to make them blame Dash."

"NO."

It was loud and angry and final. Nils only laughed in response.

Lisette's shadowy borders shuddered and grew more diffuse, and Nils laughed harder. It was bitter at first but became more unhinged and manic as he continued. He held himself as though it hurt to laugh, and he closed his eyes and sighed as he leaned back against the wall behind Hartwell and raised his head to stare at the ceiling.

"Oh my word, I had no idea," Nils said, still laughing a little.

"What the hell are you on about, Nils?" Hartwell demanded. His eyes remained locked on Ventura, even as they watered and threatened tears at any moment.

"I thought you were lying, you know? This whole time. I thought Dash was an excuse, a reason you could use to kill. I mean, people kill for all kinds of reasons, it didn't matter to me. I thought it was just a convenient lie. That you were just killing for the sake of killing. That you loved it, Lisette. And that you, Bart, just don't have the spine to defy her."

"You watch your mouth," Hartwell growled, inspiring a fresh burst of laughter from Nils.

"Of course. Of course! You really mean it, Lisette. Because you had no idea what happened."

"You're talking out of your ass, Nils," Hartwell growled. He readjusted his grip on the woman and was nervously trying to back up, inch by inch.

"It's true, though," Herbert said. "There was a ghost. It was like nothing I've seen before or since. It killed the boys. Dash just tried to help them."

"And then the thing went into the crowd," Nils continued. "It turned them on Dash. It made them believe he was the killer. Those idiots you killed were just tools. They were like robots; they didn't know what they were doing."

He laughed again. Lisette's mass of shadows was spinning and swirling in on itself. A sound like a shriek rose from deep inside.

"You spent all these years focused on sincere revenge, and you didn't even know who wronged you."

His laughter wasn't meant to be taunting, but it was. It came across as an indictment of Hartwell and Lisette, their actions, and their foolishness. Their ignorance.

"You're lying," Hartwell spat. Lisette shrank in on herself, and the shadows thickened. The blurry edges of her form hardened and became clear, even as the core of what she had become grew darker and more solid.

"You know I'm not," Nils said with a sigh. Hartwell shook his head.

"It wasn't an act. It was never an act! It was for Dash. She did it all for the boy, and I did what I did for her."

Tears fell from his eyes now, and he lost his focus. He looked at Lisette instead of Ventura, but the agent did not capitalize on the moment. Hartwell's gun was still firmly against the mother's head, and he shook profusely.

"Love shouldn't turn you into a monster," Shane said. Hartwell sobbed, squeezing his eyes shut and forcing out more tears.

"What do you know about it?"

"More than you'd think," Shane offered. Hartwell ignored him.

"What do you do when what you love is a monster? What was I supposed to do?"

"Could have told her the truth," Nils suggested.

"It was never an act," Hartwell sputtered. "She was so broken when it happened, and Artemis locked her away. He hid her away before she could find out the truth. By the time she was free again, it was too late. There was no going back."

Nils could only laugh again. He spread his arms wide and looked at Herbert, then Shane, and finally Lisette.

"You see? It doesn't matter. All those people died and none of it mattered. None of it changed anything. And none of them were even responsible. My God, how did we ever hold on to these lies for so long, Herbert?" Nils asked.

"What lies? What do you mean?" Herbert demanded.

"The lie that we are who we were," Nils clarified. "We're dead, Herbert. We're not people. You're no one's son or friend. You're a monster. I'm a monster. Just like Lisette. This is what the dead are supposed to be. Why do you think ghost stories are told to frighten children? Because we're dangerous. We're what happens when even death loses its power. We are goddamn nightmares."

Lisette howled like a wounded animal, and Hartwell shuddered at the sound. It was the sound something makes before it dies.

"I don't know what to do here," Ventura whispered.

"Nothing yet," Shane whispered back.

There was a breakdown coming, and it was impossible to guess which direction things were going. The revelation of Burkitt's influence on her son's death seemed to have broken Lisette all over again. If the first time had turned her into a shade of herself seeking vengeance, Shane was unsure what this new information would do to her.

"That might be what you've decided, but it doesn't make it true," Herbert said to Nils. "You don't have to be anyone other than who you were, and you know that."

"I don't, Herbert," Nils shot back. "I have felt it. I feel it. I see them everywhere, every day. I see these bags of meat and bone, and they have no idea what is waiting for them. The endless… nothing. Aren't you lonely, Herbert? Doesn't knowing this is meant for you, for the rest of eternity, make you crazy?"

"No."

His answer was simple and quiet, and the anger it inspired was plain on Nils' face.

"You're a horrible liar, Herbert. We both played the same stupid game. We stayed with the carnival because it was our family. You in your tent. Every day. Me at the ring toss game. Every day. And what came of it? Your family went up in smoke, and now you're alone. You will be alone forever."

"I can find new people, Nils. So can you."

"We're dead!" Nils shouted. "Who will you find? Shane? He's going to die too. Every living thing dies. I watched everyone die. But us? We will stay like this for the rest of time."

That was the crux of it, Shane saw. The death of the carnival, the death of all the people he had known for an entire lifetime, had broken Nils just as losing her son had broken Lisette. It wasn't as dark for him or as incomprehensible, but the overall effect was the same. He had lost everything.

"Everyone loses people," Herbert pointed out. "Even the living. You don't stop being a part of the world as a result."

"No?" Nils chuckled dryly and reached a hand for the woman clutched in Hartwell's arms. She could not see the ghost, but she felt the cold of his fingers on her cheek and screamed.

"Let's see how she moves on when her son is dead."

The ghost dashed from the wall and crossed the room. Lisette shrieked, the sound almost deafening. Nils passed through the wall and the shadow ran after him. Hartwell tossed the woman aside, forgotten and unimportant now.

"Don't move," Ventura ordered, approaching the man, and pressing the gun to his head. Hartwell froze, the gun still held in his hand. His breathing was erratic and fast, almost hyperventilating now. The stress combined with the fear and guilt and adrenaline was taking its toll on the old man. He couldn't keep this up much longer. Physically, he seemed to be on his last leg. He needed to put his foot down with Lisette, get her to see reason, or die.

"The woman," Shane said to Ventura. "Forget him; save her. Get her out. Now."

He didn't wait for the agent's reply. Nils was off to kill the boy and Lisette was following, which put everyone else in danger. If Nils killed the child, Shane didn't think anyone else would survive. He ran out the door after them, unsure of where they were headed.

Or who might follow him.

CHAPTER 24

BETRAYALS OF OLD

The scream came from two rooms down. Shane ran to the door and pushed it in, ducking quickly as an aluminum tray flew across the room, narrowly missing his head.

Lisette stood at the child's bedside and held two of the surgical team members in the air, one in each hand. Shane saw the flesh freeze black around her fingers in seconds. They screamed in agony, but she paid them no mind. Instead, she hurled one of them at Nils as though the body was a weapon.

The corpse passed through Nils untouched. The boy's bed lurched and crossed the room, then pulled back by Lisette's free arm. She threw the second body and again it had no effect.

Lisette put herself between Nils and the boy in the bed. Shane could see the father on the far side of the room, face-down on the floor. There was no way to tell if the man was alive, but he was not moving.

Shane cursed. Lisette and Nils were probably bound to objects Hartwell had on him. If he sent either back, there was a chance he'd be putting Ventura and the mother at risk. If he let them stay, then Shane and the boy would have to deal with them.

Shane already knew that Lisette was strong alone. He was not confident about going toe-to-toe with her a second time. He'd do it, of course, but to have Nils there as well made his odds much worse.

"What are we doing?" Nils taunted. Lisette said nothing.

"Your boy is dead," the male ghost explained. "He's been dead longer than he was ever alive. Protecting this one means nothing."

Lisette raged, and her whispers seemed to shake the walls. Shane felt the words, even if he couldn't understand them. They pulsed through his flesh and into his bones.

The lights in the room began to flicker as cold air swept across the floor. Shane swore out loud as he watched the walls vanish. Shadows danced about the periphery of his vision.

Children's giggles rose from the silent corners, playing just under Lisette's furious whispers. Nils stood his ground, intent on passing Lisette and reaching the boy on the bed.

Lisette went silent and so did everything else around them. The hospital room was no more. She had summoned the children to her aid, and with them, their ability to strip away the world and take their prey to the dark, endless places of nightmare. Places from which no one would escape, not even Nils.

"None of this means anything. Why don't you see that? After all these years, why are you still so blind?" Nils demanded.

Lisette didn't respond. Instead, a tiny form crept from the shadows and into the flickering overhead light. It was a little girl, no more than five years old. She was focused on Nils and looked at him with empty eyes. The sockets were chasms that gave a view into her skull and nothing more.

Nils was unmoved, but the girl jumped on him like a predator on prey. While Nils had been unfazed by the corpses Lisette threw, another ghost was a different matter.

Like Herbert, Nils had spent most of his afterlife in relative comfort. Though he had died traumatically, he had never gone through anything challenging afterward.

The people who worked at the carnival, Artemis Bartolomy in particular, could see ghosts. But more importantly, he wasn't afraid. Neither were the others. They welcomed their fallen friends back and treated them like nothing had happened. Nils had no idea how rare that was.

His entire afterlife had been easy. Nils and the other ghosts had not suffered after death; only Lisette had been put through that. The loneliness and confusion of returning from the dead was not something they had to deal with.

Nils did not know how to be dead. He had no idea how to handle stress or danger. He did not know how to fight because nothing living or dead had ever challenged him until now.

The ghost of the little girl was like an animal. She gripped Nils' body and slashed at him with sharp nails atop tiny fingers. He cried out, more in surprise than anything, when the girl cut open the side of his face, extending the slit of his mouth several inches on the left side.

Harm caused by a ghost to another was permanent. They could destroy each other as well as Shane could, and it was not uncommon. Shane had seen his fair share of battles between spirits that resulted in the destruction of one. The little girl was clearly going for blood.

With Nils distracted, Lisette was open. Shane knew she was still the greater danger, and he needed to put an end to her. He might not get another chance.

Shane rose on his haunches, ready to run at her when Nils' fight with the little girl was at its peak.

"Where are you going?" a voice whispered.

Shane turned to see a child's face nearly pressed to his own. A boy, older this time, with sunken cheeks and missing teeth. He lunged for Shane, cold, bony hands reaching for his neck. Shane used his momentum to roll them both over until he was on top of the spirit. He could see others congregating in the shadows and knew there was no time to hesitate.

No words were spoken. Shane held down the ghost with one hand and brought his other elbow down hard. The ghost's head split and Shane slammed it one last time, causing it to crumble and then burst.

Shane's body was thrown back, and Lisette shrieked in rage. The lights of the room began to strobe, and the illusion the ghosts created faded in and out, revealing the real world beneath it.

Lisette's body expanded, the shadows moving like bits of fabric trailing off her body in an unfelt breeze.

Hartwell appeared, drawn by her cries. He was still armed, and Shane wondered what had happened to Ventura. The older man stood in the room, overwhelmed by the flashing images of the false reality created by the children. He focused on Lisette instead, coming toward her with his hands up.

"We have to go, my love," he pleaded.

The raging whispers tore through the darkness and caused Shane's ears to ring. Nils still wrestled with the girl as another spirit jumped him from behind, an older ghost with bloodshot eyes and bleeding gums.

"It's not safe to stay!" Hartwell shouted.

Lisette's shadow spread up and out, latching onto the walls of the room, and covering the ghostly illusions. Shane watched as it took root like a living thing, spreading a layer of crystalline frost across whatever it touched.

The room grew colder and colder, and he could already see his breath forming before his eyes.

Nils took hold of the little girl's spirit, finally prying her away. He threw the ghost just as Lisette had done with the corpses of the hospital staff, except he was able to hit his target. The girl hit the expanding waves of Lisette's shadowy form. Shadow embraced the ghost, swirling around it as though trying to swaddle the small body, but the cold came with it.

The little girl writhed and dark, diamond-like ice blossomed on the ghost's face. Shane had never seen a spirit freeze another. He didn't know it was even possible.

The girl was consumed by the shadows, drawn into them until there was nothing. The illusion weakened once more.

There were gasps from the darkness as children realized what happened. The illusion ended, broken in a flash, and only the room remained.

Lisette's shadows were stuck to the walls and floor and ceiling around her. She was like a spider in a web black as tar, and Shane could see a brief flash of the real woman, the spirit unencumbered by hate and blindness. She emerged from the shadow for a heartbeat, her expression aghast as she reached for the spot where the ghost girl had vanished.

She had consumed the ghost. The girl was a part of Lisette now, gone but fueling the stronger spirit. Shane could see it was unplanned, a surprise even to Lisette. Her power was overflowing, and she had taken the girl by accident.

The realization hit with terrible force. Lisette screamed once more and more shadows spread across the ceiling. The air crackled as ice coated every surface.

Shane was on his feet again. He made a move for the boy in the bed, but Nils cut him off.

"That one is still mine," Nils hissed. He had lost his second attacker, but Shane could not see where. He must have fled when the children saw what Lisette had done. Either way, Shane had no time. He punched Nils in the throat and grabbed the end of the boy's bed.

"Shane!" Ventura yelled. He was holding the door open, something clutched in his hand as his arm came forward and released.

The chunk of iron flew from the man's hand. It passed in front of Shane, spinning end over end, and then hit Nils square in the chest as he came back to attack.

Ventura grabbed the other end of the bed and helped Shane take it to the hall and away from the ghosts. Nils reappeared only a short distance away, next to Hartwell, but the interruption was all Shane needed to get the boy out of the way.

Lisette had covered the ceiling and had nearly consumed the walls. The room had become a deep freeze, but Hartwell had not left. He stood before the central shadow, before the woman he loved, and pleaded with her to stop what she was doing.

Despite everything he had seen and the things she had him do for her, Hartwell was not giving up. He loved her despite acknowledging she had become a monster. There was nothing more Shane could think to say to him. Hartwell was a lost cause, as lost as Lisette, but still saddled by mortality.

Shane and Ventura dragged the bed away from the door. The mother was there immediately, clutching her unconscious son. Shane looked at Ventura, but the other man was focused on the room behind them.

The doors opened, but neither Nils nor Lisette came after them. Herbert appeared instead, dragging the father from the room. The man groaned, dazed from some kind of attack but still alive.

Ventura helped Herbert and lifted the man, dumping him onto the bed alongside his son. He took the mother by the shoulder and, as gently as he could, given the circumstances, pulled her away.

"We need to get them out of here," he told her.

She could only nod, her fear almost palpable. From her perspective, nothing made any sense. Unable to see the ghosts, she had no idea what had happened to the staff, why Hartwell had taken her hostage, or what anyone was talking about. All she knew was that her child had almost died multiple times and Ventura was trying to keep him alive.

"You can't have him," someone shouted. The boy from the morgue appeared just as Nils came from the room and Shane swore again.

"Ventura," Shane said. He tossed the man an iron ring, which he caught in midair. "Make it count."

The agent nervously slipped the ring over his finger while the mother helped him guide the bed away from the commotion.

Shane got in Nils' way, preventing the ghost from going after the child. He still had an iron ring in his pocket, but he would not need it for Nils. If the ghost would not stop on his own, then Shane had no choice.

"I'll kill you if I have to," Nils told him.

"Was about to say the same thing."

CHAPTER 25

ANNIHILATION

One of Nils' teeth flew from his mouth and vanished from existence. Shane punched the ghost in the face again.

Herbert tried to get his former friend to listen to reason. He pleaded and swore and threatened, but nothing worked. Nils was intent on killing the boy. To do that, he needed to kill Shane.

Behind them, Ventura had only made it a few feet before he was forced to stop. The ghosts of the hospital children were holding him at bay, preventing him from taking the family and the hospital bed to the nearest elevator.

"Help him," Shane said to Herbert, deflecting an attack from Nils. The big ghost looked back at Ventura and then at Nils once more.

"Nils," Herbert said.

"I will kill you for a second time, Herbert, so help me God," the other ghost growled. Herbert had no response. He turned his back on his former friend and joined Ventura, trying to hold off the smaller but no less dangerous horde of ghost children.

Shane could afford no time to make sure his companions were okay. He had to trust that Ventura was a quick study and that Herbert would step up in a pinch. Herbert's track record for fighting was not the best so far, but their options were limited in this situation. Kill or be killed seemed all that was left on the table.

To their right, Shane saw darkness creeping from the room they had just left. Lisette's shadow was like a rash spreading through the hospital. He had no way of knowing whether Hartwell was still alive inside. She could have killed him outright by now, or the freezing cold of the room could have done him in.

Nils rushed at Shane and ducked low, his ghostly body slipping into the floor so he could sneak under the counterattack. With a quick jab and pull, the ghost pulled Shane's feet out from under him and got him on his back.

Shane planted a foot in the ghost's gut, but it was not enough to force him back. He scurried up Shane's body and punched him squarely in the nose. Shane responded by gripping the ghost's collar and pulling him down hard as he lifted his head. He met Nils with a powerful headbutt that caused his own nose to bleed but sent the spirit reeling backward, clutching his face.

Nils was slow to react, giving Shane time to get back to his feet. He spared a glance behind and saw Ventura swing at one of the ghost children. His fist passed unencumbered through the ghost's head, but the iron ring did its work. The spirit vanished, forced to wherever it was bound.

Though Ventura could not physically interact with ghosts, it almost gave him an advantage in a fight. There was no resistance, no need to worry about his fist connecting into a hard skull or teeth or coming up short. He took wild swings and banished anything that came within range; he just couldn't destroy them. But it was better than dying where he stood.

Freezing black shadows spread across the floor like crystals of ice on a window. Nils stepped into one and his leg became rooted. He pulled but Lisette's shadow spread, covering his feet and wrapping around his ankle like tiny serpents, coiling over themselves again and again.

"No," the ghost growled, pulling his leg to free it. More shadow spun up his shin toward his knee. Shane stepped back, watching as it consumed him.

"Get me out of this," Nils demanded. Shane scoffed.

"This one's on you."

The ghost pulled at the shadowy tendrils, but they clung to his flesh and pulled his hand tight to his leg. The shadows branched there, some continuing up his leg and flowing up his arm. They moved unsteadily, jerking up to the left and then to the right, sometimes twisting and other times rising like fluid surging upward.

Nils was trapped, bent over, his hand bound to his knee and immersed in darkness.

"Herbert!" Nils yelled. "Help me!"

The big man was at Ventura's side, fighting off a teen ghost with a broken neck. Lisette bellowed, her cries louder and deeper than ever before. She had given in to her rage. Her darkness was all-consuming.

"Herbert!"

The shadow swallowed Nils' arm and was now flowing up his neck. Shane left the ghost and went to help the others. The children were fewer in number. Only a handful had stayed to fight, and Ventura was forcing them away as quickly as they came for him. The children were fighting a losing battle, and they knew it.

"Herbert, help m—"

The final word was smothered as the freezing shadow swarmed into Nils' mouth. Both his legs and most of his torso were gone. The darkness pumped into his mouth, covering his nose like the blackest oil slick, and then rolling over his wide, desperate eyes. His face was swallowed, and only his right arm remained free. In moments, it, too, was taken into the blackness.

Nils looked like the shadow of a man leaning over, cast against a backdrop of nothingness. And the icy darkness continued to spread.

The mother of the boy in the bed screamed suddenly, and Shane could not discern what had even happened for a moment. She could see none of the ghosts, but Ventura fell to one knee an instant later, blood pooling at the front of his shirt.

"Go now," he insisted, trying to keep pulling the bed even as he clutched an unseen wound. Shane came to his side while the woman began pushing. Herbert helped her, though she couldn't see, dragging it toward the elevators.

"What the hell happened?" Shane asked, pulling open Ventura's jacket.

"One of those little jerks has sharp fingers," he explained. Shane lifted the shirt and found a puncture wound just below the other man's ribs. It was small, about the size of a pencil, but he couldn't tell how deep it was. Blood flowed freely, and there was a chance it had hit something vital.

"I got him," Ventura added, holding up the ring on his finger. "I'm no slouch."

"You did pretty good for a guy who has no idea how to deal with this kind of thing," Shane agreed.

The shape of Lisette emerged. She was coming for Ventura, walking toward him slowly but purposefully. She must have seen him fighting the ghosts and protecting the boy. In her eyes, he was killing children and taking away the one she was trying to save. He was an enemy, like all the others.

Shane stepped in front of Ventura.

"If you can move, you need to move," Shane said. Ventura grunted.

"Yeah, no. Just have to catch my breath, and I'll run out of here. You'll see," he said.

Lisette stood before Shane. She had lost her boy so long ago. She had been imprisoned because of what it did to her, kept sealed away with only her anguish for company. And then she had been freed and sent on a path of vengeance, only to learn that those she held responsible were not as responsible as she had thought. She had lost everything. Her life, her child, her revenge, and ultimately, her humanity. Nothing was left of Lisette that touched the light.

Shane looked to the end of the hall, where the elevator doors had closed with a ding. The bed and the family were gone. Herbert remained. He had gotten them to safety, at least for now. Downstairs, they could find doctors again, and get free of the hospital. They could keep the boy alive. The three of them had succeeded in that, at least.

As Herbert returned, Ventura struggled to his feet. He was losing a lot of blood from the wound. Lisette came for him again as he rose, and Shane blocked her path.

"Just you and me now," he said, trying to get her attention. "We haven't really had a chance to talk yet. But you got me framed as a killer, and I'm taking that personally."

The whispers came, but the words were lost on Shane. He didn't care what she was saying, he just needed to keep her busy.

Herbert was on Ventura's side, and they began their journey to the elevator. Lisette moved to pursue, and Shane closed the distance between them. He took a swing at her.

As Shane's fist passed through her shadows, he felt cold like he had never experienced. It bit into his flesh like he was punching through acid, first itching and then burning across his knuckles and the back of his hand.

He clipped the side of her face and pain ran up his arm to the elbow, forcing him to clench his teeth to bite back a cry of pain. He pulled back and a layer of skin peeled off his knuckles, sticking to her face for just a moment before crumbling to dust.

No other ghost had caused a jolt of searing cold that went straight to his bones quite like Lisette. There was no room for a living thing in her darkness. She would freeze the warmth from anything she touched, and it would be impossible to stop her.

Shane stepped back, keeping himself between her and her prey. He did not know how to stop her if he could not touch her, but he had precious little time to come up with a solution.

Here goes nothing.

CHAPTER 26
MOTHER DEATH

Shane could not get close enough to Lisette to use a ring, and he didn't think it would matter if he did. She would return to Hartwell in the next room and be back in moments. There was no stopping her that way. She needed to be destroyed.

The shadows on the floor preceded her, and Shane kept moving backward. The pace was slow, and it seemed as though Lisette needed to consume the hallway around her before she could move forward. The wisps of darkness licked against the ceiling tiles and the walls, covering it slowly and freezing everything before she moved on.

Shane kept the pace, backing away slowly and looking for an advantage. There were no holes in her defense, no spots where the freezing black emptiness left anything clear that he could see. There was no way any living thing could get to her.

The elevator dinged behind him. Lisette hissed loudly, the whispers of her voice rolling over on themselves in a frustrated tone. Shane turned to look back, and the hallway was empty. Ventura and Herbert had left. He was alone with the ghost.

If there was a way to get to Hartwell, he still had a chance. Shane could find her haunted item on the man and bury it in cafeteria salt. He could seal her away the same way Artemis had and leave her like that forever.

Eternity in salt and sealed in lead was not a fate he would wish on anyone, but there was no other option. If she couldn't be touched, he couldn't stop her. As powerful as she was now, no one would be safe. The hospital would be shut down, but he couldn't imagine what kind of excuse they could come up with to justify it. A gas leak? Radiation? He couldn't think of anything that would hold up under scrutiny.

There had to be a way to double back. Shane did not know the floor plan of the hospital, but there could be a branch of the hallway behind him he could take, a place he could go to weave back and get behind her before she realized what was happening.

Lisette was terribly slow now. He had to use that. It was his only advantage.

Shane backed up faster until he felt he was a safe distance and then turned, ready to run. He stopped before he started. Shadows pooled in the hallway from the other side as well. The darkness had spread like flowing water along the edges of the ceiling and floor. The frozen darkness had worked its way behind, now ahead, of Shane. She wasn't moving slowly. She was weaving a trap for him to ensure he could not escape. And it had worked.

Only a few yards of space were clear in the hall. Lisette's darkness oozed outward, filling in the gaps and forcing Shane into a smaller and smaller space. He had seen how it had consumed Nils and knew it would be similar for him, but not the same. Nils could not feel the pain of freezing to death. Shane would feel it all.

Shane reached into his pocket and pulled out his pack of cigarettes. He had three left and lamented that he wouldn't get to finish them all. He took one and placed it between his lips, lighting it quickly with the Zippo.

"You know," he said, eyeing the shadow spirit as he dropped his jacket on the ground, "I almost felt sorry for you for a while there."

He pulled his shirt over his head and stood dead-center in the ever-shrinking patch of untouched floor. He inhaled deeply and exhaled a cloud of smoke at her as he tore his T-shirt in half.

"It's a sad story," he continued, wrapping half of the torn fabric around his right hand.

"But killing everyone who gets in your way really takes the justification out of the vengeance. Goes from a righteous plight to, I don't know, a tantrum?"

He wrapped the other half of the shirt around his other hand and tightened both as well as he could before punching his cotton-covered fists together.

"Let's go out with a bang, then."

He raised his right hand, fist clenched tight and protected as well as he could make it with the remains of the T-shirt. Before he could move in to take a swing, the shadows around her shuddered and collapsed.

Herbert crashed to the ground from the darkness, dragging Lisette with him. His bulk fell on top of her, and he swung like a man possessed, pounding fists into her head and body with a fury.

Lisette shrieked and lashed out, but Herbert's momentum was powerful. Though the shadows took hold of his lower body, where they reached for his arms to hold him still, he simply tore free, while slamming one fist down and then another.

Shane nearly spit out his cigarette and had to push back the urge to cheer the big man on. They did not have time on their side, and he would not get another chance like this. He waded into the shadow until he reached the two ghosts. His hands grabbed Lisette's head, and cold seeped into the fabric of his impromptu gloves.

Herbert's eyes met Shane's. Neither of them said a word. The big man kept up his assault and Shane grasped as firmly as he could, then wrenched to the left. He nearly stumbled but held fast and pulled hard.

His feet slipped from under him, and he fell back. He knew hitting the blackness of the floor would burn through his back in an instant. But he did not let go. Shane's hands, already burning from the cold, gripped with every ounce of strength he had.

Lisette's head separated from her body. The structure and shape of it warped. Shane's hands came together, and the head crumbled between them. It burst, exploding out with a force that sent Shane and Herbert flying in opposite directions.

Shane hit the ground hard. The tile floor was cool but no longer frozen. He stared up at a light fixture, white bulbs behind frosted glass. There was no more ice or darkness.

Pain still filled his hands and his fingertips felt like there were razor blades in them. He lifted his hands and looked at his exposed fingers, angry red and almost blue around the nails. But they all still moved.

"Shane!" Herbert cried out. "Shane, are you okay?"

Shane lifted his head. Herbert was slumped against the wall next to the operating room. They looked at each other, and Shane laughed.

"Herbert, you beast!" he yelled back. The ghost grinned and rubbed his chest and stomach.

"That was crazy," he said. "But there's no damage to me, I think."

Shane laid back again, staring at the ceiling once more.

Neither of them moved for a long while. Finally, Shane could hear Herbert getting to his feet. The ghost came to his side and looked down at him on the floor.

"Are you injured?" he asked.

"Oh, probably," Shane replied. His hands felt like they were on fire, and he must have bruised a few ribs. It had happened often enough that he was good at self-diagnosing.

"Ventura got away. He's downstairs. A doctor is attending to his wound."

"That's good," Shane said.

"And the child will be okay. They finished his surgery before Lisette and Hartwell got to him."

"Hartwell," Shane said. He needed to make sure the man was gone. He grunted as he sat up slowly, wincing as he did so. It took him longer than he would have liked to get back to his feet, and when he did, he wanted to lie right back down.

Herbert walked with him, keeping a slow pace. They entered the operating room side by side, but only just. There was no need to go farther.

Bart Hartwell's body was on the floor, sitting up against the wall. The gun was on the floor next to him and there was a hole in his chest through his heart.

"He shot himself?" Herbert asked. Shane shook his head.

"Not a gunshot," he said. The wound was through the breast pocket of his shirt. It must have been where he kept Lisette's haunted item against his heart. When the ghost was destroyed, the item followed suit. The explosion was enough to send shards of the tiny comb into his heart and kill him.

They stared at the body for a moment. Shane lit another cigarette and turned around.

"Let's go," he said, staggering toward the elevator.

"Go where?" Herbert asked.

"Anywhere," he answered.

Herbert said nothing and helped him to the elevator.

CHAPTER 27

THE ROAD AHEAD

Shane and Ventura sat on the back of the same ambulance. Shane's ribs had been wrapped and his hands bandaged with ointment for the frostbite he'd suffered. A doctor assured him he would likely fully recover, but his hands would be numb for a few days.

Ventura had been stitched and bandaged and was also expected to recover in no time. More FBI agents and state police had arrived, and he was forced to put on his professional persona once more. He spun lies artfully, pinning the incident on Bart Hartwell and an unnamed accomplice who broke out through a sub-basement previously thought inaccessible.

The APB on Shane was scrapped, and Ventura made a note about the invaluable aid he'd rendered during the investigation. Shane would have preferred not to have his name mentioned at all, but Ventura did it anyway.

"You handled that well," Shane said. Ventura snorted.

"Not really. Local police chief doesn't believe for a second that anyone escaped through a sub-basement, and no one seems to know how a rickety old fart like Bart Hartwell burned off everyone's face. But it'll be a cold day in hell before someone comes up with a more reasonable explanation that they can prove."

"As long as no one is looking at me," Shane said.

"You're good. Least I can do for you," Ventura said, including Herbert in the statement as well.

"Don't sell yourself short, Ventura. You saved that kid and his family. You fought off a small army of bloodthirsty kids from beyond the grave. That's a solid day's work."

"Yeah," Ventura agreed. "Speaking of..."

He lifted his hand and took off the iron ring, handing it back to Shane.

"You can keep it," Shane suggested. The other man shook his head.

"Doesn't fit right. Think I might make something a little more practical, anyway. One that doesn't require me to get as close."

"If you like," Shane replied, taking back the ring.

Ventura was pulled away to answer some questions. The hospital officials were busy getting the patients back to their rooms and the staff back to work. The scene was disorganized, but Shane didn't think there was any other way it could have gone down.

"You're quiet," Shane said, lighting another cigarette. Herbert looked at him and half smiled.

"Guess I'm just not sure what to do now. It's over, but I have nowhere to go. Where does a homeless ghost go?"

Shane inhaled deeply and narrowed his eyes.

"What are you talking about?" he asked.

Herbert was confused.

"I just mean, I'm not sure what to do now."

"No, before that. We're not finished," Shane told him.

Herbert didn't understand, so Shane pointed off in what he thought was the right direction.

"Burkitt is out there someplace. All of this, every death back to Dash, and I bet plenty before that. All of it happened because of Burkitt. I'm not leaving things like that."

He took another deep inhale and let it out, squinting at Herbert through the cloud of smoke.

"You don't have to come," Shane said. "But I could probably use a hand, and I figure you've got more skin in this game than anyone."

Herbert's face split into a smile.

"When do we leave?" he asked.

Shane held out his empty pack of smokes.

"As soon as I can find a store," he said.

EPILOGUE

The wind was colder than it should have been for that time of year. It flowed through the skeleton of an old house and howled through cracks and crevices. Even though it was midday, it gave the impression of a terrifying old nightmare home from a movie.

Outside, a man stood in the road. A length of bramble vine was wrapped about his ankle, but he paid it no mind as he shuffled slowly up the street. The clothes he wore hung in tatters, punctured and shredded unevenly over his body, the fabric stained reddish-brown and black with blood that had long since dried.

His flesh was no different than his ruined garments. Strips of torn, dried skin hung from his face and deep, scabbed-over scratches covered every exposed inch.

The deepest of the scratches, like a ditch cut into his face, went from his hairline across to the jaw on the opposite side, digging through his left eye in the process. The wound was damp-looking and festering, oozing pus and infection, especially at the swollen eye that was little more than a mangled mess in his skull.

Some scratches still had embedded thorns from the brambles he'd been trapped in. Others were simply caked in old blood and dirt. They looked angry and painful, and in the deepest parts of his memory, the bramble ghost knew they had been. It had been painful when he died. He had been alone and terrified and in so much pain. But that was the way of things in Burkitt.

The ghost ambled away from the howling house and the tangle of thorny shrubs that held his long-since-rotted corpse. He walked toward a place near the center of the town of Burkitt once known as Magister's Hill.

A house sat atop Magister's Hill, the oldest house in Burkitt. It had been built in the late 1600s by a Dutch settler who left the colony behind to branch out on his own and forge a new life for himself and his family. A doctor by trade, he had once entertained dreams about taming the wilds of the new world and bringing science to the savagery of that place.

No one in Burkitt knew the name of that settler, and not everyone believed the house was that old. It had changed hands many times over the years. The British once took over the land, and then the Quakers after them, and during periods of turmoil, owners were known to disappear and leave the home vacant until someone new discovered it there on the hill.

There was no town of Burkitt until the mid-1700s. The house was just a stop on a trade route for many years before that. A place where travelers might sometimes stop in the cold of winter hoping to find a friendly face and a warm bed for the night. Some people found those things, some did not. Everyone found something, though.

Thomas Aldridge Burkitt moved into the house just four years after America became a country. He had to repair the rundown property, and he helped found the surrounding community, the place that would become Burkitt just a short time later.

When Thomas Burkitt died of cholera, his son Samuel took over the property for only a year before his untimely death. He was found in a shed behind the main house, his tongue and eyes missing. But the town of Burkitt continued to grow.

Soon, the magister's house was used as the mayoral residence. That tradition was abandoned less than a decade later, after Mayor Bradley Crawford's family died there. Each was found hung outside of their window with a sheet about their neck.

Magister's Hill had been owned by businessmen and lawyers and doctors and several others over the years. Few stayed long. Some left suddenly, unable to stand another night in the house. Some went mad there. Some died. Some simply vanished.

The town of Burkitt paid little mind to the goings on at Magister's Hill. It was rural Delaware, and life was not easy for anyone in those days. People died from disease, hunger, accidents, and more. The town of Burkitt learned not to care. The people there held that deep disinterest in their hearts. Generation after generation of them were raised to turn a blind eye to suffering, even as the ill fortunes of Magister's Hill flowed out into the rest of town.

The bramble ghost had died many years ago. He did not know how many because his mind no longer worked in a way time could touch. He didn't exist in a time and place so much as in feelings. He was trapped in his pain and suffering and loneliness. The bramble ghost had been in Burkitt forever, as far as he knew. He had been tormented for all time there. He could not remember anything before.

Other ghosts watched him shamble down the street. They hid in their own shadows and suffering. They watched with dead eyes, bloody faces, or faces that were missing entirely but still, somehow, they watched. All the spirits of Burkitt could see what happened inside Burkitt.

None joined the bramble ghost. None called out to him, even those that recognized him or knew who he had been before the thorny branches of the skeletal house had wrapped around him like serpents and peeled the flesh from his bones.

This was not the first time one of Burkitt's dead had made the journey to Magister's Hill. Many traveled to the looming, dark structure after years in the town took their toll. Even the dead could be pushed too far.

The house on the hill was wide and tall. The siding, added by some later owner, might have been red once, but years of the elements had turned it a dark charcoal with red hints around the windows that glared out like unblinking eyes.

Eight windows on each of the three floors made the broad front wall look like some kind of angular spider. When the sun hit it right, the light reflected off each surface, and it looked like panels of blinding fire were staring back at the town.

The door was redder than an apple, and the paint seemed immune to fading or chipping. It was the only part of the grand old house that looked forever young. The rest was blotchy and peeling and as old as the hill on which it sat.

"I'm tired," the bramble ghost said at the foot of the hill. He craned his ragged neck to look up with his one functional eye.

"I'm tired!"

None of the other spirits of Burkitt spoke. Some receded into the darkness, not wanting to remain so exposed. They knew what came next.

"I'M TIRED!"

The ghost's voice carried far and was dry and painful to the ear. He began to walk again, slowly and deliberately, up the stone path along the hillside to the door of the house. The length of bramble trailed behind him, twisting of its own volition now and then as though trying to take root.

No ghosts hid on the hill. None would dare get so close. They remained in the town, beneath the shadow of trees and in the hollowed-out spaces in homes that were as dead as the ghosts.

No one had lived in Burkitt for more than thirty years now. Some had left, realizing the town was a lost cause, and packed up their homes and families and went out into the world. If they survived or thrived, no one in Burkitt could say. The dead only knew of the things that remained with them. There was no longer a world outside of Burkitt for any of them.

The bramble ghost struggled up the hill. He was a spirit and therefore experienced no physical discomfort. He was not too weak to make the climb. He could not be. Despite that, the journey weighed on him. Burkitt pulled at him, as though the town needed him to return to his post at the skeletal house. But he would not go back.

He reached a plateau at the top of the hill and could stand straight once more. The ghost stared at the red door.

"I don't want to be here anymore."

He spoke to the door, to the house itself, but no one answered him.

"I DON'T WANT TO BE HERE ANYMORE!"

There was no reply. The bramble ghost's throat rattled, a sound like the last gasp of a dying man, and he scowled.

"End it, you coward."

The wind rustled tree leaves, and the bramble ghost swore. He raged and slammed a fist against the red door. It held firm, like a door struck by a living fist. The ghost hit it again and again, pounding his hands against the blood-red wood. Still, nothing answered his calls.

In time, his fury wore thin. He had shouted every curse he knew and created twice as many more. The house offered no apology or attack. It was like all the other homes in Burkitt. It did nothing.

The ghost turned. He headed back down the hill, limping and shambling with an awkward, unsteady gait.

Clouds passed over the sun above him and cast moving shadows along the long-abandoned streets. The breeze sent a shushing sound through the treetops.

As the ghost reached the bottom of the hill, one of the shadows drew itself up. It pulled away from the tree that cast it and gained bulk and dimension. It changed from a simple spot on the ground to a solid thing birthed from that darkness.

The bramble ghost stopped and stared at the thing blocking his path. It was not darkness; it was merely in darkness. His one eye focused on the face of what waited for him.

"What is this?" the ghost whispered. He took a step back, and the breeze became a gust.

Branches swayed violently, and the shadows danced across the street. The thing that had been born from them moved as they moved, and soon, it was not there. Like an illusion, it faded from sight and there was nothing more to see.

The bramble ghost turned to look at the house but could no longer see it. The dark form was blocking the view now, so close they were touching. He turned to stare into its face. His shredded, dry lips parted, but he said nothing.

The dark spirit stood at the base of the hill. It was still like a statue carved into the shape of a man. But there was a face there, with eyes that looked out at Burkitt and saw all the ghosts in the darkness, those who hid and those who didn't. It saw them and knew them.

Those that dared look back at the dark spirit knew it, too.

But there were only a few who did so.

Check out these best-selling series from our talented authors:

GHOST STORIES

RON RIPLEY
BERKLEY STREET SERIES
MOVING IN SERIES
HAUNTED COLLECTION SERIES
DEATH HUNTER SERIES

IAN FORTEY
JIGSAW OF SOULS SERIES
CULT OF THE ENDLESS NIGHT SERIES

SUPERNATURAL SUSPENSE

A. I. NASSER
SLAUGHTER SERIES
SIN SERIES

DAVID LONGHORN
NIGHTMARE SERIES
ASYLUM SERIES

SARA CLANCY
THE BELL WITCH SERIES
BANSHEE SERIES

For a complete list of our new releases and best-selling horror books, visit ScareStreet.com or scan the QR code below!

www.ingramcontent.com/pod-product-compliance
Lightning Source LLC
Chambersburg PA
CBHW050400030726
47503CB00006B/1943